MAYO GHOST

Kieran Ginty

1

Published February 2014

ISBN 978-0-9575571626

This 1st edition printed and bound in the Republic of Ireland by:

Lettertec (Irl) Ltd, Springhill House, Carrigtwohill, Co. Cork, Republic of Ireland

www.selfpublishbooks.ie

AUTHOR'S INTRODUCTORY NOTE

This fictional story is set in the year 1996. The predominant locations are Dublin and Mayo. In pre-Celtic Tiger Ireland, the children born from 1970 onwards are beginning to make their mark in the big bad world.

However, there is another world which some of them have experienced, and some of them have not. And some of them have experienced it without even knowing it. The world of ghosts.

Whether you believe in the paranormal or not, I hope you enjoy this tale. Many readers use books to help them to go to sleep at night. It is my intention that this book stops you from sleeping!

This book is dedicated to all who supported me and read my debut novel 'The Boys of Ballycroy'. I sincerely thank you. But this is a new story, largely unconnected. Please give yourself some time to get to know the two main characters in the first few chapters – then you will be taken from there....

Kieran Ginty
February 2014

CHAPTER 1

Friday 4th October 1996

The whizzing sound of cars speeding past Lucan's Spa Hotel buzzed in the ears of the 20 year old hitch-hiker. His focus, of course, was on the traffic leaving Dublin City and after half an hour of 'thumbing' he was having no luck. He was beginning to feel frustrated. He had earlier decided to miss two lectures in order to get an early start on his journey back home to Mayo.

The 5 feet 11 inch student cast a glance at the overhead skies. Despite earlier showers, the day was holding out and the rain that threatened from the dark clouds hadn't made his situation worse. The sun was winning the day's battle overhead. It was nearly 2pm. His blue rucksack lay flopped between his white Adidas runners. That morning, he had considered the possibility of scrawling a sign with 'Castlebar' written on it to help get 'a lift' from one of the thousands of cars which would surely be making the trip into the west from the capital, but he felt that his navy Mayo GAA Football jacket would suffice. Surely a fellow Mayo person would have sympathy for him and pull in?

He brushed his right hand through his brown hair as he extended his left arm. His thumbs-up sign would surely yield dividends soon. He peered ahead of him, bracing himself for the possibility that a fellow 'thumber' would arrive and take up a more advanced and favourable position. He was in no mood to tolerate any competitor if one should appear.

As he glanced again up at the skies he suddenly heard the screeching of car brakes in front of him and he breathed a sigh of relief as a large cream car slowed and eased into the hard shoulder, its left indicator flashing. He yanked his rucksack up from the tarmac. There was a glare from the road as the sun reflected from morning rainfall and he peered again to examine the car which had now ground to a halt about ten yards away.

"Oh yes! And it's a Merc!" he muttered to himself as he opened the left hand side rear door, noting the registration number of the car: 96-MH-2013.

"Come into the front if you like" said the driver, whose face he had not laid eyes on.

"I will, but I'll just throw this old bag in the back!" replied the grateful student, before thinking to himself "This must be a rich fecker, it's some car."

As the traffic continued to whiz by, the young Mayo man caught a first glimpse of the driver. Except that, it turned out NOT to be his first glimpse – as he recognised the face! However, it appeared that the driver did not recognise his new passenger.

"Thanks a million. I'm Sean" said the student, settling into the comfortable front seat. He tried not to stare too much at the driver, who was paying more attention to the rear view mirror as he prepared to rejoin the main flow of traffic heading west.

"I'll just pull out here...just wait a minute...ah, here we go" said the driver as he revved up the cream Mercedes-Benz and got back to the pace he had been going when he spotted the hitch-hiker.

"Sean, is it? I'm Thomas" smiled the driver. "Sure I couldn't pass by a fellow Mayoman!"

"Plenty must have passed me!" came the reply. "Fair play to you."

"Just promise me one thing" said the driver continuing to smile, "There will be absolutely NO mention of the replay loss last Sunday, OK?"

"Fine by me!" said Sean. "It has been one hell of a long depressing week!"

"So let's not depress ourselves then, agreed?" smiled Thomas, "Where are you heading for?"

"Castlebar" replied Sean.

"Great!" came the response, "I'm passing there so you are on the pig's back."

"Far from a pig this car is, it's a beauty! What a machine. And a '96 reg as well!" said Sean, surveying the impressive cream leather interior. "I know we are not to talk about the All Ireland defeat, but aren't you taking a risk by bringing a Meath car into Mayo?! This week of all weeks!"

"I suppose I am, Sean" came the reply, "But it's not mine. It's the boss's. And he offered it to me for the weekend – and sure how could I turn it down?!"

"How could you is right. It's SOME car" enthused the student. "I hope it's well insured though!" Both men laughed.

As they edged further west, Sean took a moment to retrieve some chewing gum from the pockets of his blue jeans to share with Thomas. He looked again at the driver. It was definitely HIM, the scar over his left eye was the giveaway. Sean had noticed it when he spotted Thomas in The Portobello Bar some months earlier. Despite attempts to cover it with a wavy parted fringe, the scar was visible. Today was his THIRD day seeing this man, and it was already obvious that the man had not recognised him in return.

As both men commenced chewing their gum, Sean reflected to himself on the two previous occasions he had seen Thomas. He wondered if he should mention it to him – perhaps it would sound weird. It's bad enough telling a girl you have seen her before, but telling a bloke was chancy. And they had a three hour journey ahead!

The man with the scar had made his 'mark', so to speak, with Sean because on both occasions he was in the company of a good looking woman – a different one each time! Initially, of course, it was the blonde companion in The Portobello who had caught his attention. She was a stunner. Every man in the pub must have noticed her, in her little maroon dress. And of course they all had wished they were in the shoes of the tall smiling Mayo man. Why wouldn't he be smiling with such a babe hanging off him?!

Sean had been with his own pretty girlfriend Yvonne that night in The Portobello, but that did not stop him admiring the other talent. Now, that lucky fecker was right beside him, driving a magnificent Merc! "Some guys have all the luck!" he told himself.

And just two Sundays earlier, on the day of the drawn Mayo versus Meath match, Sean had recognised the same man in 'The Big Tree' pub in Drumcondra, but this time he had a taller brunette with him! Both she and Thomas were wearing green and red Mayo jerseys. As with the night in The Portobello, Thomas was sporting a wide white smile, and his floppy hair again failed

7

to hide the scar on the edge of his forehead. What helped imprint Thomas into Sean's memory was the fact that he looked very like the actor who played 'Scarecrow' in the TV series called 'Scarecrow and Mrs King'. The same actor also played the main role in another TV series, 'Bring Them Back Alive'. Sean decided to mention the similarity:

"Has anyone ever told you that you look like yer man from 'Scarecrow and Mrs King'?" asked Sean.
"Bruce Boxleitner, you mean?" laughed Thomas, his teeth sparkling. "Yep, I get that ALL the time. Wish I had ALL his money though!"
"You're the spit of him!" laughed Sean, relieved that he had not offended Thomas. "I bet it helps when chatting up the women!"
"Not that I need any help there!" laughed Thomas. "Did you know that in real life Bruce Boxleitner is married to the actress who played Laura in 'Little House on the Prairie'?"
"Really?" replied Sean.
"Yep. Melissa Gilbert. She's MY wife!" laughed Thomas.
"That's gas!" Sean replied. "Mrs King must be very jealous!"

"My father's side came from Holland near the border with Germany, so I often wondered if there might be an old connection with the Boxleitners somewhere along the line" said Thomas, chewing. "Maybe they were in the concentration camps together!"
"You would wonder alright" answered Sean, "Maybe so. So you are from Dutch stock. Where do ye live now?"
"I'm from Ballycroy, do you know of it?" replied Thomas, in the typically Irish way of answering a question with another question.
"Everyone's heard of the 'The Boys of Ballycroy', haven't they?" replied Sean in a similar fashion. "Wasn't that a film or a book back years ago?"
"It was both!" answered Thomas. "And my great-grandfather is one of the main characters!"
"Really?" responded Sean. "The man from Holland?"
"No. The Dutch are on my father's side. Sylvester McDonnell, from the novel, he's on my mother's side and that side are 100% Irish I assure you!" smiled Thomas.

"Wow. We're not even in Enfield yet and you are putting me to shame! You have a super car; you look like a movie star; you are married to Laura Ingalls Wilder and your great-grandfather starred in a novel and film!"

Both men laughed again. It was clear that the two Mayo men had 'clicked'. This journey would pass quickly.

"What is your surname Thomas?"
"Goy" was the reply. "G-O-Y. It used to be Van Goy when my grandfather came over but we shortened it."
"Goy from Ballycroy!" exclaimed the student, as he looked out on the flat green grasslands of Meath.
"Indeed" replied Thomas. "And what about you, what's your surname?"
"McRobert" answered Sean.
"Anything to the vet McRobert, I cannot remember his first name?"
"He's my uncle, Charles. You know him so?" asked Sean.
"He used to be the vet for my father's farm down in Ballycroy. Nice man. Must be retired now?" asked Thomas.
"No, still going. My father was an agricultural inspector, but he covered mostly the south of the county, so you probably don't know him" said Sean.
"No" answered Thomas. "So what are you doing in Dublin, are you following them into the farming game, keeping the McRobert line going?"
"Not really. I'm studying to be an Environmental Health Inspector in Cathal Brugha Street" came the response.
"Good for you. Good game to get into" replied the driver.
"And what game are you into yourself, it must be a good number?" asked Sean, again surveying the car's luxury interior with admiration.
"I'm into a lot of different bits and pieces" smiled Thomas, "But at the moment it's computers. The boss has made his millions already, and I'm trying to follow!"
"Really?" replied Sean.
"Yep. He's from Meath but based in Dublin. He has gangs of us going all round the country teaching people how to use the internet, I am sure you are familiar with it?"

9

"The world wide web!" asserted Sean.

"Indeed" replied Thomas. "That's my game at the moment. Good money in it. EVERY thing will be done through it in the future, so everyone is trying to come on board now. The boss is making a mint!"

"I can see that!" laughed Sean. "Interesting stuff."

Just as they were leaving the outskirts of Enfield, Sean felt himself being suddenly thrust forward as Thomas pressed down hard on the brakes and the shrill sound of the car skidding could be heard. The seatbelt hurt Sean's chest as they came to an abrupt halt.

"Fuck!" cursed the driver, turning red with rage, his smile now replaced by a look of utter anger and hatred.

In front of him, Sean could now see the reason why they had to brake so hard. A small red Nissan Micra had pulled out in front of them from a left side lane in Enfield, with the intention of getting across to the opposite side of the road to drive towards Dublin. Thomas had not been expecting the car to shoot out in front of him, and he just missed ramming into the wing of the Nissan by an inch. The male African driver looked meekly at Thomas, and lifted his right hand to acknowledge his mistake, whilst at the same time edging his little car closer to the white line on the middle of the road to get into the contra flow of traffic.

But his half-apology wasn't working with Thomas who was losing his temper and was irate. Sean noticed beads of sweat appearing on the forehead of his new friend, who was winding down the window in anger.

"You fecking idiot!" he roared. "What the feck are you doing you black bastard?!!"

Sean was taken back by the reaction. He had never seen Bruce Boxleitner lose his cool like this!

"You fecker, you fecker!" repeated Thomas, blowing the car's horn angrily with his closed fist, and leaning out the window.

The African did not help the situation by pursing his lips and pointing his index finger to them, as if to say "silence". This agitated Thomas even more. Luckily for the African, an oncoming driver had flashed his lights to allow him escape the tricky situation.

Thomas went to get out of the car to confront him before he drove away, but Sean instinctively grabbed him by the left arm.
"Don't! He's not worth it!" shouted Sean.
Thomas looked angrily at his passenger. He glared at him, and went to say something but decided against it. Sean was right. He needed to calm down. The cars had not collided.

Sean drew back his arm.
"Take deep breaths" he said to the older Mayoman.
The cars behind the Mercedes began blowing their horns, so Thomas took one final deep breath before releasing the handbrake and heading into the empty lane in front of him. The glare of the sun from the wet road was dazzling them both.
Thomas finally broke the silence:

"That was just too bloody close!" he muttered.
"It was. The dick-head!" replied Sean, trying to re-ingratiate himself with the driver and attempting to retrieve the atmosphere they had enjoyed before the Nissan frightened them.
"Excuse my language but that fecking black bastard..."
"Stop!" interrupted Sean. "At least you did not hit him. The boss's car is OK. No one's hurt."
"No thanks to that African fecker!" said the annoyed Thomas, before going off on a hate-filled rant:

"And it would have been my fecking fault if I had hit the bastard. I HATE them! I really DO! That car was probably handed to him by the state, which probably pays for his petrol as well! And he smiles at me and points to his lips! Who the feck does he think he is, the bastard? That's what we fecking get for sending them all those Trócaire boxes! They used OUR pennies to fly over here and take our jobs and our houses and our cars and our women! That's what they fecking did. They should all just fecking feck off back to..."

"That's enough Thomas, come on now" interjected Sean. "Listen, pull into the petrol station up here and I will get you a Lucozade, you could do with a drink"
"Something stronger than Lucozade is what I need!" replied Thomas, indicating left into the forecourt, as the smile came back to his face. He wiped the sweat from his brow as Sean left the car. Sean too was feeling hot, and took off his Mayo GAA jacket and threw it into the back seat on top of his rucksack.

Within minutes, the conversation had started up again as the 20 year old and 25 year old continued their journey west, imbibing to replace the energy they had just lost!

"That's two topics now off the agenda," laughed Sean, "The All-Ireland and Africans! All that's left now to discuss are 'Work' and 'Women'!" The smiles were back.....

CHAPTER 2

As the duo left the town of Kinnegad behind them, they both fully recognised that they shared more or less the same sense of humour. They had definitely bonded and the journey was passing fast.

The younger of the two was quickly growing in admiration of the driver, and tried not to stare too much at the scar on Thomas's forehead. It looked like a birthmark, but he could not be sure. He wondered again if he should raise the fact that he had sighted Thomas twice previously in Dublin bars, but again opted against it. He looked on with envy as the IT Trainer answered two calls about work on his mobile phone. Not many people had such an apparatus, this was the closest Sean had ever been to one.

He noticed the creaseless chinos and expensive-looking navy shirt that Thomas was wearing. He considered himself as being scruffy in comparison, but after all he was just a student. Even the rich whiff of Thomas's aftershave was impressive.

As the Mercedes-Benz overtook a bus that was also heading westward, Sean thought to himself how lucky he was being chauffeured in luxury instead of being cramped in an uncomfortable bus seat. But Thomas's next comment was to bring him back to reality:

"I'm taking Monday off and am working in Sligo Tuesday, so unfortunately I won't be able to give you a lift back. Perhaps another time – I will give you the mobile phone number when we get to Castlebar."
"No bother. Thanks. Sure this is just fine" replied Sean hiding his disappointment.

Music – mostly from the 1970's and 1980's came from the stereo and whenever a song either of them liked came on Thomas raised the volume from a button by the steering wheel. Not that many males would admit it, but they both hummed along to songs by The Pet Shop Boys and Chicago!

In between, when the volume was turned down, they continued their conversation and spoke about their families. They learned that they each had only one sibling – Thomas having a younger brother and Sean having a younger sister.

"You mentioned your great-grandfather from the novel – how come he was in it?" asked the passenger.
"Well, he and his brother were murdered in it." replied Thomas.
"Really?"
"Yep. Afraid so! He and his brother fell foul of a man who held a gripe against them since the war. So he had them beaten up and thrown in a lake to drown. Tied to a weight. They were never found."
"Bloody hell!" replied Sean. "Ballycroy must have been rough!"
"It actually happened near Newport" replied Thomas. "And to this day people reckon they have seen the ghost of Sylvester on the Newport to Mulranny road!"
"Get away!" replied Sean in astonishment.
"Yep. Plenty have seen him. They say he carries a teddy bear. They say he had a teddy bear with him when he was killed. He had it for his young kids. Sure my grandmother was less than a year old when he was taken."
"The poor creatures" said Sean. "They were violent times. But sure, you don't believe in that ghost craic, do you?"
"I fecking do!" came the firm reply.
"Really?"
"Listen. Maybe there once was a time I felt like that but no more" asserted Thomas, looking serious.
"And why 'no more' – did you see a ghost?" asked an increasingly curious Sean.
"Kind of. More of a presence. A spirit. Enough to make me believe that there is another world out there!" said Thomas.
"Come on, tell me!" begged his passenger.
"Maybe later, not now" replied Thomas, his eyes fixed straight ahead on the road as Sean took another look at his scar.
"Ah come on!" repeated the eager Castlebar man.
"Maybe later. It's very personal, it's...it's not easy to describe. I will need to compose myself. Only a handful have been told. It's not easy at all" said Thomas, arousing even further the curiosity of his companion.

14

When he heard the distinctive tones of Bob Dylan coming through on the stereo, the uncomfortable Thomas took the opportunity to try and change the topic:

"I'm turning this up. 'Positively 4th Street' – my favourite from Dylan!"

"Never heard of it" said Sean, slightly disappointed that Thomas has not elaborated on his story.

"Just listen to the lyrics. And the tone" said Thomas smiling. "What a bitter song. How he captures the hatred. You can feel the contempt he feels" he added before unimpressively singing along to the song.

Sean nodded in agreement as he absorbed the lyrics, and Thomas's singing grew louder as the verses continued. Despite the poor effort at singing, Sean was impressed by Thomas's knowledge of the song and began thinking to himself "why can't I come up with a song that nobody else knows! How come he has such insight? He is only five years older than me but makes me feel like I know very little. I can't wait to hear his ghost story!"

As Dylan's offering came to a close Thomas was snarling along to the final verse:

"Yea I wish that for just one time you could stand inside my shoes, you'd know what a DRAG it is to see you!"

"What a tune! What a tune!" Thomas gasped as the song faded and he reduced the stereo volume to get Sean's reaction.

"Good alright" was the verdict. "A bitter and angry song, as you said."

"I'd love to write a song like that!" said Thomas. "He's a genius."

"But you could never be THAT bitter I'm sure!" responded Sean.

"Me?! Me?! You don't know me!" laughed Thomas, making eye contact with his passenger. "I am THE most bitter person I know!"

"Get away!" laughed Sean. "Bruce Boxleitner could never be bitter!"

"Listen. My motto is this…" offered Thomas as Sean paid full attention, finding it hard to believe that the happy demeanour of the Ballycroy man could cloak any bitterness. "Don't just get even – get ahead!"

"What?"

"Yep. That's my motto. 'Don't just get even – get ahead!' Not only will I always gain revenge if someone wronged me, but I would go one-up on them."

"Ah, I'm sure you haven't been wronged too often anyway" remarked Sean.

"That's not the point. And I HAVE been wronged" stated a serious-looking Thomas. "But anyone who has got on the wrong side of me has ended worse off, I assure you!" he added.

Sean tried to lighten the tone of this latest segment of their conversation:

"The African is in for it so!" he laughed but the reply he received was a cross one:

"I thought that topic was off the menu!"

"I'm just saying...." uttered Sean half apologetically before Thomas jovially tapped his passenger with his left hand.

"I will give you some examples in a few minutes of how I have gained revenge and more on people who have dared to wrong me" added the driver as he speedily overtook another car.

"Good!" replied Sean.

"My favourite lyric of ALL time comes from the end of the David Bowie song 'Ashes to Ashes'" said Thomas as he shuffled himself in the ultra-comfortable driver's seat in preparation of regaling his examples. *"My Mama said, to get things done, you better not mess with Major Tom."*

"Bowie must have written that especially for you Thomas!" laughed Sean.

"I often thought that!" replied Thomas, repeating the lyric.

"You know what Confucius said?" offered Sean, glad that he was able to come up with a suitable quote. "He said that 'when you set out on the journey for revenge, dig two graves - one for yourself!'"

"That's shite!" uttered Thomas. "No, 'don't just get even – get ahead! That's the ONLY way. And now I will give you some of my examples."

Sean sat deeper back into his cosy seat as the church steeples of Mullingar came into view. He was looking forward to finding out even more about his new-found friend...

CHAPTER 3

"The barony of Erris is one of my favourite places on earth, and I have many friends there, but one night an eejit from there was bothering me in Geesala Dance Hall. I tried to keep out of trouble but he followed me to the toilets, where he head-butted me. I STILL don't know why, I could not understand what he was saying as he was fairly pissed. He thought I was spoiling his chances with a woman he had eyed up or something. I had a fair bit of drink on me too, and was dazed by the head-butt.

The following weekend, I saw him again in a disco in Belmullet and this time he was sober and acted as if nothing happened. He got a nice surprise I can tell you when he went to drive home from the disco that night as all four of his tyres were slashed!"

"Good on you!" said Sean.
"And not only that, but I could see his farm across the channel from our parish; about two miles away as the bird flies. And a week or so afterwards I could see that they had got their silage done – you can tell by the colour of the field. So, to 'get ahead', my payback was to pepper his silage cover at night with pitchfork punctures as he and his parents slept!"
"Wow!" said Sean in admiration, as Thomas grew more enthusiastic in imparting his tale.
"So, their silage rotted and they had to dump it all – and spend thousands on buying in replacement fodder for the livestock. That got him back for his stupid head-butt!"
"And they never found out it was you?!" asked Sean.
"He accused me alright but he had no proof! I just smiled at him. And that was the last bother I ever got from that gorilla!" laughed Thomas gleefully.
"You are true to your word!" said Sean. "Remind me not to get on the wrong side of YOU!"

"And another time, there was this girl who stood me up for a date in Belmullet one night and I got a fair bit of slagging as of course I had boasted to everyone that I was going to shift her!" said Thomas, now 'on a roll' and eager to impress his companion, and show him that he was a man not to be messed with.

17

"I was willing to let it go, seeing that she was a lady and all of that, but she slagged me off to another girl and that made me mad. So the next night that I met her in Belmullet I was prepared. I brought with me a little one of those tubs of Chambourcy chocolate mousse, and smudged it all over the arse of her white trousers – you could always guarantee that she would be wearing white trousers – when I was passing by her and before long the whole pub was in stitches as it looked like she had had an accident!"

"You fecker!" said Sean, laughing as he tried to picture the incident.

"And she never showed her face in Belmullet for another six months" laughed Thomas. "And to top it off, I started going out with her former best friend not long after that! Boy, did them two women hate each other or what!"

"You are some fecker!" said Sean, in admiration as they both chuckled. "Any more revenge stories?"

"This is the best one" said Thomas, struggling to contain his zealousness. "There was this tosspot at home who was stuck into everything – you know the type – always organising things and getting to know everyone's business and being in every community event photo that was ever taken. A real busy-body. Into sports, cards, darts, raffles, grave-digging, EVERY THING. But a single man – sure of course he would never have the time to marry or rear a family he was so busy minding every one else's business! Well, he took a dislike to me. I could see through him. I never genuflected in front of the fecker. The self-anointed 'Pillar of Society' – more like 'Pillock of Society!' I must have been the only one to see what a sad nosy sod he was.

He used to referee football games all over the north of Mayo and also submit reports to the newspaper. One day in a match I scored 2 goals and 2 points and to spite me he never even mentioned me in the paper – and credited the goals to his nephew who couldn't score in a brothel! I was irate. Sure of course I had told the whole family of my exploits and I can still see the image of my poor father thumbing through the newspaper to proudly read about his son's 2 goals and 2 points. I wasn't even mentioned! He then thought I was lying! Thankfully some people who attended the match backed me up.

Well, I showed that fecker! Firstly, just to get even, he came home one evening to find his two prize-winning dogs poisoned. As dead as dodos!"

"No!" exclaimed Sean in shock.

"I am telling you, Sean, NO-ONE messes with me and gets away with it. And the poisoning part was just to get even!"

"What did you do to get ahead?" enquired the Castlebar man anxiously.

"Well. I wasn't long compiling a nice dossier on him for the Revenue Commissioners, detailing the brown envelopes he was getting for refereeing matches, for sending reports to the paper, for working as a bouncer in night-clubs, and for giving lifts to old isolated people to the post office for them to collect their pension – a nice slice of which went to him. Within weeks the Inspectors were out and he had lost his medical card AND his dole!"

"Jaysus!" exclaimed Sean. "That was SOME revenge! But did he find out it was you?"

"He didn't have to – my smile when I next met him said it all!" replied the laughing driver. "And the sad fool couldn't do a thing about it! But, if he had not wronged me, he would have been fine. He has never been the same man since, rarely rises out now at all. Let him stay inside his shell - it's his own fault" ended Thomas displaying no sympathy or regret.

Silently and privately, Sean felt slightly sorry for the nosy man. But it was clear now that Thomas – despite his outwardly friendly and harmless demeanour – had a very dark side to him and was certainly not someone to be messed with.

As Thomas continued to smile and turned up the volume for another one of his favourite tunes, Sean began to feel just a tad uncomfortable from the thrill that Thomas was obviously getting from other's misfortune. However, he envied the confidence and ability of the Ballycroy man to put wrongdoers in their place. Maybe 'don't just get even – get ahead' was a motto he would have to adopt himself. Maybe it would help him get that little bit of respect he craved, especially at college. Among his fellow students, he was a poor Mayo man who never stood out from the crowd. And here beside him was a man from a 'lesser' background than he who was showing who ruled the world. His wandering thoughts were interrupted by a question as they crossed the border from Westmeath into Longford:

"Have you any stories of revenge, Sean, you MUST have?!"
"Let me see..." was the reply as Sean struggled to come up with something. Nothing immediately came to mind. He tried to think again, to delve deep to the back of his mind...
"Surely in college there must be something!" said Thomas. "By the way, have you a girlfriend?"
"I have – Yvonne – from Clontarf" he mumbled as he continued to dig into his mental memory bank.
"Here's one!" he said as Thomas smiled in anticipation. "It's not as good as your stories but..."
"Go on!" urged Thomas.
"Last year, this tosser of a landlord refused to give us our deposit back on our student house in Drumcondra. One hundred quid each he owed us, and we were relying on that for our end of year drinking session. He made up some yarn about us damaging the garage door but we all swore it was damaged the day we arrived."
"The bollix!" interjected Thomas.
"I know!" replied Sean, "So on our final day we went to the fishmongers and bought as much mackerel as we could afford, and we stuffed the fish wherever we could – cisterns, pipes, under floorboards...and the best one: into the hollow curtain rails! We reckon he STILL hasn't found those!"
"Brilliant!" exclaimed the impressed Thomas. "I must tell that to Norman, my housemate, in case we don't get our deposit back in Ranelagh!"
"You KNOW a person named 'Norman'!" replied Sean cheekily. "I thought that name went with the flood!"
"He wouldn't like to hear you say that!" said Thomas. "What about Norman Whiteside? Norman Mailer? Norman Wisdom?"
"Wisdom?!" laughed Sean with incredulity, "Who the hell is Norman Wisdom?!"
"I forgot – sure you are only a young fella!" laughed Thomas.

"And just to finish up on the landlord" added Sean, "We heard he had to gut the house and not only has he no students this year, his neighbours have none either because of the stench! So he is NOT Mister Popular!"

"It goes to prove what I said" stated Thomas. "If he had been fair with ye he would not have suffered that misfortune. In my book, fairness equals fairness. Unfairness equals awareness – as revenge will be sweet".

"Didn't someone say 'Revenge is a dish best served cold'?" said Sean, delighted to produce another quote from up his sleeve.

"And serve not only the dish, but dessert too I say!" said Thomas as he overtook a small car that had slowed down in front of them. "Don't you just hate cars that slow down on inclines – you'd swear the driver had to peddle up them!"

As the cream coloured Mercedes-Benz glided towards Mayo, the elder of the two turned up the volume and they unashamedly sang in their best high-pitched voices to the sound of Bronski Beat's 'Smalltown Boy'. Only two males very comfortable with each other's company could do that!

As the speed increased, so did the respect and admiration Sean had for his new-found friend. Over the next twenty or so miles, that level was to increase even further as Thomas relayed some of his experiences from outside of Ireland, an island that Sean had yet to ever leave...

CHAPTER 4

"Ah go on, will you tell me about your ghost experience" begged Sean.

"Listen" asserted Thomas, "When we cross the Mayo border I will tell you. I don't want it to dominate the rest of our drive. As I said, I need time to gather myself. My friends have observed that my voice starts to change whenever I discuss what happened, like I sound like a different person."

A shudder ran down Sean's spine.

"Thomas, there really is no need to tell me if it's that upsetting, really" he emphasised.

"No. I will tell you. I trust you. I know you won't take the piss!" replied Thomas.

"I have actually written a book about a ghost story set in Mayo" he continued.

"Really?!" responded Sean, gobsmacked. "You have written a book?!"

"Yep. But it has not been published yet or anything" answered Thomas, focusing his eyes as usual on the tarmac in front of him. "It's in draft form, ready to go, but I have been a bit slow in getting it advanced any further. The new job has taken up too much of my time. But I'm meeting the owner of a publishing house in Dublin this day week. We'll see how it goes."

"Wow" said Thomas. "I am sitting beside an author! Is it fiction or fact?"

"Well, most people would say that ANYTHING to do with ghosts is fiction, but I have done it as a novel, with various characters in an old folks home – dying and coming back to haunt each other and all that kind of stuff. There are a few twists in the story. That's about all I can say. No one knows about it – not even my parents - so don't be telling anyone in Castlebar you got a lift from an author or anything – a few people in that town know of me and I don't want to ruin my 'street cred'!"

Sean swayed his head in amazement. This guy was only five years older than him, yet he was packing so much more into his life. He felt like he was still at the starting blocks whilst the Ballycroy man was on his twentieth lap! Surely it should have been the other way around – with the McRoberts being 'townies' and the Goys being farmers. He was simply stuck for words, but Thomas had even more feathers to add to his cap:

"I have been writing bits & pieces since I was in Inter Cert. Poems, songs and stuff...and now of course the novel. My dream is to have enough money to be able to retire early and move to Paris, where I would write more and more every day."
"Amazing" said Sean. "Paris. Imagine that!"
"I've only been there once" added Thomas.
"You've been to PARIS! You lucky fecker. I give up!" laughed Sean. "Let me off here in Longford, you are starting to depress me now!"
"Ha ha!" beamed the driver. "Don't despair. You are young yet. When you get your degree it will be your passport to the whole wide world! You will be able to go wherever you wish! Where's the first place you would go to? And don't say Longford!"
"New York for sure" replied Sean without hesitation. "That's where I would LOVE to go!"

"It's some city alright" replied Thomas.
"Don't tell me you have been there too?!" said Sean, looking across at his smiling companion.
"Yep. Several times!" giggled Thomas almost embarrassingly. "Sure I lived in the States for two years. I went there when I was twenty. But I decided to come back. I was an illegal alien and it wasn't worth the risk."
"You're mad!" said Sean. "But lucky!"
"You are probably too young to appreciate it, but there is no country like Ireland. You better get yourself down to my part of the world. Mulranny, Achill, Ballycroy and Erris – they are all beautiful. Scenery you wouldn't find anywhere else on earth. Fresh, heather-scented sea air. And decent people..."
"Other than those who head-butt you and don't list you on match reports!" intervened Sean.
"Beautiful Mayo called me back – as did a beautiful Mayo girl – so I left the U S of A behind me!" sighed Thomas.
"And probably a few broken hearts" laughed Sean. "What part of America were you in?"
"Cleveland mostly" came the reply. "It was grand, but not for me."

"And what did you work at over there?" asked Sean.

"Ah, different bits and pieces. Landscaping. Security. I got myself into the office of the security firm and it was there I taught myself about computers. And it was from there that I sent some of my compositions to record companies."

"Did you have any joy?" asked Sean tentatively. He should have known the answer would be in the affirmative.

"Well, I got one break alright where a singer took on one of my songs. Did you ever hear of Sue Silkberry?"

"No. Can't say I have" responded Sean.

"She's fairly well known over there, has collaborated with KD Lang and Willie Nelson and a few others."

"And you wrote a song for HER!" exclaimed Sean.

"Well, yeah. She took it on. Made a few changes, and offered me ten thousand dollars for the rights if I signed them over" said Thomas.

"And did you?" asked Sean excitedly.

"Of course I did! I nearly bit her hand off!" laughed Thomas. "That paid for my fare home and helped me get set-up in Dublin. In fairness, even though she takes credit for the song, she mentions me in the acknowledgements of her album on which it appears. I will show it to you sometime, it's in my own car."

"This takes the biscuit!" gasped Sean. "I mean...where is this going to end? You will be telling me next you wrote the last three Eurovision winners for Ireland, and that you appeared in Father Ted, and that you have a winning lotto ticket in your wallet!! EVERY thing you touch seems to turn to gold. Are you having me on?" Thomas could not contain his hearty laughter, as he tried to concentrate on navigating past the bridge at Tarmonbarry that brought them across the shimmering Shannon River from Leinster into Connaught.

"It's true!" he chortled. "I will show you the album. The song is called 'Die in Ohio' and is about an American soldier in Vietnam who just wants to get back home - alive."

"Did it chart?" asked Sean.

"The album did well, but it was never released as a single. She probably made a million from the album sales so the ten thousand I received was nothing to her."

"Amazing! Wait until I tell the lads this when I'm golfing tomorrow, they won't fecking believe me!" said Sean, almost exasperated. His companion could not stop himself from laughing, he was finding Sean's reaction so amusing.

As they neared Strokestown it was Thomas's turn to make Sean take a fit of uncontrolled laughter. He pointed out a forest on the outskirts of the town, and a heavy wooden gate that led into it.

"There's a fella from here who I gave a lift to one day. I'll never forget him. He pointed out that gate to me and told me that a local girl called Mary McGillycuddy brought a fella from Longford there one night, where they parked up their car for a bit of courting. After an hour or so, another couple unfortunately chose the same spot for the same activity, and didn't they crash into the back of Mary McGillycuddy's parked car! All four of them had to be brought to hospital. And the joke doing the rounds in Strokestown was that Mary McGillycuddy was rammed from behind – and then a car hit her!"

Sean reacted deliriously to the joke and had to bend over his seatbelt from the laughter! When he finally managed to regain his composure, he peered at Thomas through his red, tear-filled eyes.
"Wait until I tell the lads this!" he managed to mumble.
"It's a good one, isn't it?!" laughed a scarlet Thomas, also in tears.
"I will think of that every time now that I pass Strokestown!" was the reply.

As the tearful twosome advanced through the rustic townlands of rural Roscommon, Thomas began taking deep breaths. The time was near for him to tell the story that Sean ached to hear. And this story would not at all be a funny one...

CHAPTER 5

Thomas topped-up his borrowed car with petrol at a station on the edge of Ballaghaderreen. He bought himself a large bottle of water – as he knew his throat would run dry when he was telling his story. Sean was treated to another bottle of Lucozade.

As he returned to the car with the refreshments Sean could not help but admire the fit physique of the man who was about his height, but much broader. "It's no wonder women flock to him" he said to himself.

As they left that town Thomas took a swig from his bottle and then drew a deep breath.
"I have to give you a little background first, Sean. It was May of 1989. I was preparing for my Leaving Cert. Even though I was 18, I was still eligible to play for the Ballycroy minor team. We had reached the North Mayo final. Our trainer had us doing evening running sessions on our local strand, Doona Sandybanks. No road goes all the way to it; so we usually cycled as far as we could go, and then parked up our bikes. For the remainder we had to cross over fields and ditches, and then walk through a rough path that was not conducive to cycling. Normally, you would meet a team mate or two, and travel to the shore with them."

Sean noticed that Thomas was beginning to hyperventilate. He was taking deep breaths. He seemed capable of only short sentences. Sean felt that he could almost feel Thomas's heart beating.
"Take your time. No hurry" he urged the storyteller.

"One evening, I was ambling along, as usual. Tailing a group of four of us. On our way to training. Walking. On that rough path. Between two wired fields. The sand dunes in sight, a quarter of a mile away. I carried my gear-bag across my shoulder. Whatever happened, it slipped off my shoulder. It rolled into a little drain, that ran along the field's border fence to my right. No one took any notice of my gear-bag falling. I knelt down. And reached down for the bag. To pull it back up from the drain. It was well within my arms reach.

Suddenly, I just froze. It's hard to describe. It was like I became a statue of pure ice. I was paralysed. I could not move a thing. I felt as if I was reaching for the bag, but I wasn't. I could not move my arm. I felt ice cold. Colder than ever before. I could see my bag. I could hear the lads chatting away ahead of me. Then, I felt this presence. I was overcome with sadness. With a feeling of desperation. My eyes were transfixed on where my bag lay. I felt as if I was being drawn down into the drain. I felt terrified. I did not know what was happening. I felt I was about to leave this earth. But not only that, but that I was about to be dragged to a much sadder place."

"Jaysus!" said Sean as he himself felt his spine go ice-cold.

"I did not know what to do. I tried to yell to the lads for help, but nothing came out. Then, without reason, everything returned to normal again and I was OK. I went to move my arms and they moved. I went to say my name and I heard it. I picked my bag up and stood up. I was fine. The paralysis has gone just as quickly as it came. But I felt weird. A bit dizzy. Something compelled me to look back at the spot again where my bag had fallen. There was nothing significant about it. There was a lump of rushes, a few stones, and only a trickle of water running by in the drain.

I wondered what the hell had happened. The experience felt like it had lasted about five minutes, but the lads were just a couple of yards further ahead and so it had lasted only a second or two. I caught up on the lads. I did not mention anything. How could I? They would have laughed at me.

Obviously, I did not enjoy that training session as my mind was bothered. I wondered if someone was buried there; perhaps a famine victim. But I tried to put it out of my mind, thinking perhaps that I was about to come down with a 'flu' or maybe that I was studying too much."

"Did you pass that spot on the way back?" asked Sean.
"I did – and everything seemed normal. But I made sure I wasn't alone, that I was in the middle of a group. So I was afraid I suppose."

Thomas took some more water. He was still breathing heavily and purposefully. His eyes were transfixed on the road. Sean had noticed that his voice had become a little hoarser. The joy had gone from his eyes. They now looked fearful. His complexion had turned pale. Sean himself felt he needed a drink and so he gulped some. Thomas composed himself for the next part.

"That night, I went to bed as usual. After some study. The study was helpful in putting it out of my mind. I shared a room with my brother Anthony. We had two single beds, side by side. Only three feet apart. Him closest to the window, me closest to the inside wall.

As I was drifting off to sleep, all of a sudden, the icy cold feeling returned. It paralysed me again. And so quickly. I hadn't even a chance to sit up. I was lying. On my back. Facing the ceiling. And I was SO cold. I felt dead. I felt as if my blood had frozen. I felt that I was all white – my skin, my hair, my nails, my eyes, my lips.

There was definitely a presence. A presence that wanted to invade me. A sad, desperate presence that made me want to cry. That made me want to get help. I tried to move my head sideways to see Anthony but I couldn't. As far as I was concerned, I was moving my head, but nothing was happening and my eyes were zapped to the ceiling. Again, I thought I was about to die. I roared. At the top of my voice. Hoping to wake Anthony. But there wasn't a stir from his bed."

"Fecking hell!" whispered Sean as he took another mouthful of Lucozade. Thomas's voice was now trembling. His hands were shaking as he held them out to keep them on the steering wheel. He was beginning to perspire.

"Although I could not exactly see her, I could sense that there was a little girl present. By the side of the bed. To my left. In between Anthony and me. In my minds eye I could make her out – about 7 years, long scraggy hair, sad eyes. The best description I've used is that she looked like that girl from the 'Les Miserables' posters, do you know the one?"

"I know it" croaked Sean. His voice too was becoming hoarse from the tension that filled the car. He too was beginning to sweat, as he felt his companion's intensity.

"The girl was there. By my bed. I kept roaring, thinking it would wake my parents. But nothing was coming out. I tried to reach out my left hand to wake Anthony, but my hand didn't move. I tried to kick off the blankets, but my legs remained still. I was SO cold. Totally paralysed. With fear. SO cold.

Then an image came into my head. My mind was brought back to the spot where the bag had fallen earlier. It felt again as if some force was trying to suck me into that drain. That the girl present in the room was trying to pull me in. Then, it got worse.

Starting with my toes, it felt as if she was taking over me. It was horrendous. It was like she was taking slow control over my cold body."

Thomas helped himself to another drink.
"Jaysus, are you OK?" asked Sean. "Maybe you should stop the driving. You are shaking, man, and you are sweating like a pig!"
"Now you see why I was reluctant to tell you! And now you can see why I believe in ghosts. Why I have written about them! I'll be fine." And with that Thomas took another mouthful. His throat was drying up as he recalled the ghastly ghostly experience.

"Inch by inch, she took over me, working slowly up my body. I felt I was becoming her. I was terrified. I continued to roar until I felt I was hoarse. And it was a sad, mournful, throaty roar. I felt I was in my final minutes.

"Her presence started advancing up my stomach. I thought when it reached my heart that it would finish me. It passed my heart. But I was even more terrified at that stage. I felt that once she got to my head, that that was it. That I would be hers. That I would be in her control. That my life was over. I was so frightened. Her presence was filling me with awful lonesomeness. Like nothing I had ever felt.

I waited in vain for my brother to respond to my calls. I wanted to touch him. To say goodbye. And to check that he was alright, that this spirit wasn't taking over him too.

Then came the turning point. I started to pray. In my mind. Before she reached it. Before she got into my head. She was now in control from my toes right up to my throat. I felt smothered. I felt as if I was gasping for air. That her spirit was about to conquer mine. I prayed like crazy. I begged God to save me. She continued to advance, but her presence started to weaken. The more I prayed, the more weak her presence became. She had not passed my chin. My prayers were fighting back. God was saving me. Then – all of a sudden – she went!"

"Fecking hell" said Sean, totally captivated. "Are you alright?"
"I'm fine" responded Thomas, forcing a smile, and wiping the sweat from his forehead before taking more water.
"I'm ice-cold myself here!" shivered Sean. "What a fecking experience. You poor man!"

"I got up out of bed and turned on the light. I checked Anthony and he was sleeping OK. I was expecting my parents to charge into the room wondering what the hell all of the shouting was about. But no one came. I felt as if my voice should have been hoarse, but it was fine in the morning. I waited for someone to mention something at the breakfast table, but it was a normal morning. Obviously, I never slept that night. Or ate my cereal.

The event dominated all of my thinking for the next few days. I could not eat, drink or do anything. I couldn't study. It ruined my Leaving Cert – not that I ever planned to go to college anyway. And it ruined my chances of winning the minor football title. I feigned an injury and stopped training. There was NO WAY I was passing that drain again!"

"And who could blame you?" stated Sean, feeling hoarse. "What did you think the story was – that the girl was buried there or something?"
"Exactly!" responded Thomas. "That's my theory. That she was perhaps a young famine victim and that my gear-bag landing on

her grave must have disturbed her spirit or something. She was so sad. I am still not sure if she was trying to drag me back into her world, or if she was using me as a method of returning to this world."

"And did you tell anyone?" asked Sean.

"I didn't. I couldn't. Not then anyway. They would have probably sent for the men in white coats. I wanted to tell my parents but how could I? They would have thought I was a looper; that I was on drugs or something. I wanted to tell the football coach and my head teacher – both of whom felt let-down by me. But I couldn't. It was five years before I told anyone."

"You poor sod!" said Sean. "Jaysus, I've never heard anything like that. My spine is still tingling. You poor sod!"

"But there's more!" replied Thomas, just as Sean was beginning to feel comfortable again.

"Before I left Ballycroy she visited my room twice again. And each time, it was prayer again that fought her off. I really thought my hair would be grey by now, because fighting with her presence took so much energy out of me and stressed me so much. Again, I always felt I was gone pure white, including my hair!"

"Fecking hell" replied Sean, struggling for words.

"And when I left for England and America she followed me again, trying to take me over at night. Several times. Each time less terrorising as I knew my prayers would win. But only if they were genuine, heart-felt sincere prayers."

Sean was awe-stricken.

"So when was the last time she visited?" he asked.

"About three years ago, in America. But I paid a priest over there a couple of hundred bucks to say a week of Masses for victims of the Irish Famine. And I went to each Mass. And lit a candle for the girl. Hoping that her soul might rest, and that it might leave mine alone. It has worked so far. But I still pray hard to God that she leaves me be."

"Wow. I don't know what to say!" stated Sean. "You handled it well. You're some man. I can see now why you left telling your story until the home straight. That changes the mood BIG time!"

31

"Well, you DID ask!" laughed Thomas. "Listen, it's history, I hope, and don't be thinking about it. Maybe she chose me as I am a weak person, I don't know. But the whole thing taught me not to be dismissive of those who believe in ghosts. On top of that, it has made me a better Catholic – despite my cursing and tales earlier of not only gaining revenge, but getting ahead! Maybe it's God's way of getting even with me?"
"I just don't know what to say. I'm just...dumb!" uttered Sean.

"You're not dumb. You're a sound man. And we're only 20 miles from Castlebar. So let's check the radio again!" said Thomas.
"It will probably be 'Ghostbusters' playing!" laughed Sean.

As the Meath registered car hurtled towards Mayo's hurting capital, the new friends took a break from talking and listened to tracks from Talking Heads and Wet Wet Wet – or "Cinn Cáinte agus Fluich Fluich Fluich" as Thomas translated into Irish! Sean began to feel warm again as he neared his home town. But he had a feeling that he might have nightmares later on!

CHAPTER 6

It was just after 5.30pm when they reached the 'Welcome to Castlebar' sign. Their three hours together had been remarkable. Sean had so much to digest from the trip. He smiled to himself as he realised he had found a new friend. A kindred soul. A new hero.

"It's a pity I cannot bring you back to Dublin this time, but another time for sure" said Thomas. "And don't be expecting this limo every time – my old Volvo is twelve years old!"
"I really enjoyed the lift – and the chat" said Sean.
"When we stop, I will give you the number for this mobile" Thomas said. "Just give me a call whatever weekends you are travelling. If I am coming to Mayo you can be with me. If I happen to be staying in Dublin, then I'm sure you can find an alternative way. Fair enough?"
"That's very kind of you" replied Sean as Thomas steered the car through the narrow streets, where red and green flags still drooped almost mournfully on the sunny October evening.

"So, you want to be dropped off at your grandfather's house, just give me the directions" said Thomas.
"I'll be fine here by McGoldricks Bar, you can pull in here, thanks a million" said Sean as the Ballycroy man indicated left and edged into a vacant spot directly in front of the pub. By now a few passers-by had noticed the gleaming beauty of a car, and when they noticed the registration plates they wondered if someone was arriving to gloat about Meath's victory!

Once they had pulled up, Sean reached over his right hand to shake the right hand of the man who had delivered him safely to his native town.
"It has been a total pleasure, Thomas!" he smiled.
"Indeed it has!" replied the beaming driver. "May we meet again!"

But as he opened the passenger door the Bruce Boxleitner look-alike had one more piece of news for the younger man:
"Sorry for dominating the conversation. I suppose I am on a bit of a high because...well, this is a big weekend for me."

"How do you mean?" enquired Sean, thinking perhaps that it was a birthday.

"Well" said Thomas with a bit of hesitation, "Well...you see...I plan to 'pop the question' to my girlfriend tonight!"

"Well fecking hell!" responded a delighted and surprised Sean. "Put it there again – CONGRATULATIONS to you! And to 'the missus'! Why didn't you mention earlier...you...you rascal you!"

"Well" replied Thomas, "I'm not even sure she will say yes..."

"Of course she fecking will!" interrupted the Castlebar man.

"I haven't told anyone" added Thomas "Only her father knows. It's her birthday on Monday and that's why I'm off. I want us to put a deposit on a house and then try to book a date for the wedding."

"Well she's in for some birthday!" said Sean. "Fair fucks to you. You are SOME man! I feel like I have just starred in a James Bond movie! You have me spinning from all of your action, so you have! Near misses, a racist attack, driving a Merc, writing a song, writing a book, scoring loads of goals, travelling the world, seeing a ghost, a mobile phone, a class job – Jaysus, next thing you will start speaking Chinese and tell me you have a consignment of cocaine in the boot or something!" Thomas had a good laugh at that.

For a mini-second, Sean cast his mind back to the two separate occasions he had spotted Thomas in Dublin pubs – once with a blonde and once with a brunette! He wondered how this handsome rogue who seemingly had two women 'on the go' – was going to commit the rest of his life to someone. He decided to discretely probe!

"Well – what is her name? And is she blonde, brunette or bald?!" he asked.

"Her name is Ursula and she's a stunning brunette!" came the happy reply. That gave Sean food for thought!

"Listen, I better head" said Thomas. "I just want to say..."

"No, no – hold off! Don' tell me you really ARE Bruce Boxleitner!" joked Sean.

"You're gas!" chortled Thomas. "No, seriously, I just wanted to say not to heed any of my 'don't just get even – get ahead' stuff as you are a nice lad and it's not for everybody – just for vindictive people like me, OK! Come up with your own motto and we will discuss that the next day. OK? I'm sorry again for yapping non-stop, your poor ears must be ringing, and I'm not usually so painfully chatty...."

"No, no! Don't you dare! It was a pleasure. I enjoyed every minute!" insisted Sean. "It was like a roller coaster ride! Really. My girlfriend told me that I am predictable and boring and now I can see she is right..."

"Don't be saying that!" Thomas interrupted. "You are NOT boring. Anyone who plays a prank like the fish-in-the-curtain-rail one is not a bore. You are a broke student. It will ALL change for you. But don't change yourself for ANYONE! Now, as the song says, I have to 'Hit the Road Jack' so enjoy your weekend!"

Sean shook hands with Thomas one more time before opening the door and getting out. He said nothing as a feeling of sadness came over him. It was like he was saying farewell to a loved one. He felt himself gulp. There was nothing more he would have liked than to have a pint or two with Thomas in McGoldricks, to continue their conversation that he had enjoyed so much. He opened the back door and reached in for his rucksack and jacket. He grabbed them quickly and closed the door. He gently tapped the top of the Mercedes twice to give the signal that he was clear of the vehicle. As the right indicator came on, Thomas knocked one final laugh out of Sean as he boosted the stereo to maximum volume as the chorus of Depeche Mode's 'Never Let Me Down' played. The noise drew looks from pedestrians as the cheery chauffeur headed up the town's main street in his Meath Mercedes-Benz.

Sean trooped the couple of hundred yards to his grandfather's house. Within seconds he had gone from a high to a low, and then he rose again when he remembered the laugh they had singing along together. And he laughed even more when he recalled the Mary McGillycuddy joke. His grandfather didn't, though!

After spending a couple of hours in the company of his grandfather, he rang his mother to collect him and he spent the rest of the evening chatting with his parents by the home fireside.

35

As he had an early start to join his friends golfing the following morning, he was in bed by 10pm.

The thoughts that spun around inside the head of the 20 year old made him smile. They weren't thoughts of his nice girlfriend Yvonne, or of his recent drinking sessions in Dublin, or of the prospect of meeting up with his friends on the green. They were the thoughts of a smiling Thomas – his adventures, his humour, his resourcefulness. As Sean grew more tired he continued to smile at the images he formed in his head of Thomas boring holes in the silage cover at night, of him smudging the girl's arse with brown chocolate mousse, and of him scoring two goals in a football match. Then he remembered the fear on Thomas's face as he told his ghost story. The next image he visualised was of Thomas kneeling by the standing brunette, and looking up at her, placing a sparkling ring on her finger. As he drifted off, a feeling of jealousy came over him. His sleepy smile disappeared and was replaced by a frown as he felt that he was losing his new friend as soon as he had found him, to a woman, who would take him away and turn him from an exciting man into a boring man. Who would always sit in that passenger seat beside him. Who would take him from the city he thrived in and chain him to a parish to wither. Who would occupy him with chores and children instead of letting him continue his adventures in Paris and New York.

Before long Sean was asleep. Dreaming deeply. What a day! He would never again look on life the same way....

CHAPTER 7

Saturday 5th October 1996

Sean had an early start at Castlebar Golf Club, where he participated in a game of foursomes with three of his male friends. Despite the pleasant sunny morning, Sean felt a bit groggy, a bit down. He could not understand the reason why. It was as if he had a slight hangover – and alcohol had not passed his lips the night before.

His friends remarked that Sean was not quite himself, and his poor form over the first nine holes proved it. He shrugged it off, saying he was just a little tired. He perked up for the second nine holes, and a smile appeared on his face as he hit a couple of tremendous shots and started to redeem himself.

To his male friends, Sean was a decent bloke. The typical 'sound man'. He was considered 'bright' and 'studious'. He was tall and thin, with short brown hair and pleasant enough features. He had no shortage of female admirers, but unlike many of his peers he was always totally respectful to females. He was never one to brag about his 'conquests'. He enjoyed his few pints but always knew when he had enough, and he never experienced any loss of memory from his drinking. After a couple of drinks he always loosened up a bit and became chattier, but he was never a loudmouth. His friends and family enjoyed his sense of humour. Golf and snooker were about the only sports he played. He was though, interested in many other sports including Gaelic football and soccer. The only activity he had ever won prizes for was chess – and his mother proudly displayed those trophies on the McRobert mantelpiece.

His grandfather, parents and sister loved him dearly – and always appreciated the fact that he travelled home to see them every weekend. Many students opted to stay in Dublin at weekends, but he always enjoyed coming to Castlebar – except when the Mayo team were playing a match in the capital. He was considered a loyal and caring son, brother and grandson.

To females, Sean was not exactly categorised as 'a fine thing' but he was rarely without a girlfriend. He had a couple of exes in the town who were still friends of his. His latest belle, Yvonne from Dublin, had visited Castlebar once. An auburn-haired sweet girl with a slight slender frame, she was a classmate of his, and she still lived with her parents in Dublin. She managed to stay a couple of nights each week with him at the house he shared with three other students in Drumcondra. Their courtship had surpassed the year mark, and they got on well as a couple.

That Saturday morning on the lush green acres where golfers found their paradise, Sean shocked his companions by changing his game completely and shooting an excellent final 9 holes to take the glory. His demeanour changed from being glum to being giddy, and by the time the four friends sat down for some cold beers in the clubhouse he could not stop himself from beaming.

He attributed his 'conversion' to the great laugh he had the previous day with the man from Ballycroy who gave him a lift. He quoted some of the jokes and some of the vindictive stories that Thomas had told him. The three friends laughed along for the first couple of stories but that petered out as it appeared after ten minutes that they were in for hours of chat about this guy that they knew virtually nothing about. They wanted to talk about women and football – and their planned night out later – and not about someone from Ballycroy whose boss happened to lend him his fancy car for the weekend!

"So, when are you meeting her – I mean him – again?" laughed Jamesie.
"Can a man not speak of his admiration for a fellow man without being deemed a homo?" replied Sean as the others giggled. "I DO have a girlfriend you know, ye jokers!"

The subject changed pretty quickly as the foursome caught up on the happenings of the past week. Of course, their mood became depressed when they had an in-depth discussion about the Mayo loss in the All Ireland final replay. Sean thought to himself "How right Thomas was to rule this out as a topic yesterday."

Sean remained in a buoyant mood for the rest of the day as he met up with a few more friends for a couple of games of snooker and some slot-machine action in the arcade. He smiled several times as he recalled his enjoyable trip from the day before. He wondered how Thomas's proposal had gone. At one stage he looked at his mobile number that he had written on a business card in his wallet, and wondered if he should ring him to see if the girlfriend has said "yes", but he shrugged off the concept as being possibly 'too weird'.

After the arcade, his friend Teeko brought him for a spin around the town in his orange Opel Manta, a car the young owner had 'souped up' himself in his role as an apprentice mechanic in his father's garage. As the two men put on their best poses, the beat of the 'trance music' from the car's music system reverberated through the streets. The earlier clubhouse pints had loosened Sean's inhibitions and he coolly waved to any familiar figure he spotted, lifting the elbow that was perched out of the passenger window. When he sat with his parents and sister for dinner at 5pm, it wasn't the beat of that music that went through his head, but words from a song by The Pet Shop Boys that he and Thomas had listened to some 24 hours earlier:
"When you're young you find inspiration from anyone who's ever gone and opened up a closing door."
They echoed through his mind repeatedly. And they made him smile.

Later that evening, as Sean sat in his bedroom putting on his socks and shoes for his night out on the town, it suddenly struck him why he had been so off-form that morning. As often happened, he recalled a dream that he had the night before. It was a dream that had sunk to the back of his mind once he woke that morning and became consumed with his plans for the day. The dream was of Thomas, sitting on the edge of Sean's bed, crying! Sean sat upright and closed his eyes, trying to remember more about the dream. Even that minor recall was propelling him back into miserable form.

"Gosh, that was so real last night" he said to himself as his mind tried to retrieve more. He threw himself back on the bed, with his eyes still closed, to see if it would help, and it did. In the dream, Sean himself sat up and asked the crying Thomas what was wrong. But Thomas just kept his head buried in his hands, his elbows resting on his knees, sitting right at the end of the bed on the edge. And that was it. That was all Sean was able to recall.

But now he was feeling depressed. The dream felt so real. He knew for sure that is why he was in such bad form that morning, it had affected him. It was affecting him now too.

Sean improved his mood by recalling the sing-along that they both had to the track by Bronski Beat, the two of them endeavouring to destroy their vocal chords by trying to imitate the falsetto tones of Jimmy Somerville. "Gosh, if anyone had seen us!" Sean said to himself as he fixed his denim shirt in the mirror. It was Yvonne's favourite shirt. He wished she was there to join him right now. He felt like he needed one of her warm hugs.

That night, a gang of eight comprising of five males and three females did a pub crawl of Castlebar. The Humbert Inn, The Castle Inn, The Bungalow, Hennellys, Byrnes, McGoldricks and Rockys were all visited. Sean enjoyed a bottle of Budweiser in each of them, and was well in control of himself as usual as the night drew to a close in Coxs Bar, where the music blared past midnight.

Then, a strange thing happened. As he was using the urinal in the late bar, Sean was certain he had heard the name 'Thomas Goy' being mentioned by someone at the door. He turned around and saw a couple of people there. He tried to hear the rest of the conversation but it was drowned out by the combination of the loud music plus an unfortunately-timed flush of the toilet. By the time Sean had zipped himself up and given a rushed wash to his hands, he could not find the person who had mentioned that name. He wondered if he could have been imagining it? But he was certain he heard it. He would have asked the speaker if he knew Thomas Goy too. But within seconds Sean was being embraced by a drunken mate and he forgot the incident.

It wasn't long before the student was drifting off to sleep in his cosy bed, helped by the effect of his bottles of beer. It didn't even cross his mind that Thomas might visit his dreams for a second night running...

CHAPTER 8

Sunday 6th October 1996

Sean had a hangover. His head throbbed. He received no sympathy from his parents or his sister as he tried to eat his cereal. He was due to join them for 11am Mass as usual.

As he contemplated what lay ahead of him that day, he did not even think of trying to recall what had just featured in his dreams! Mass, trimming his grandfather's hedge, phoning Yvonne, the soccer match on Sky TV, asking his father for some more cash, the bus to Dublin, getting rid of the headache – that's all that was on his mind. It was enough.

The Sunday newspaper rustled as his father skimmed through it, before his mother Joan raised the volume on the radio as usual at 10am for the obituaries on Mid West Radio. His sister was dolling herself up for church. Sean was concentrating on eating his breakfast, and wondering if he had Paracetamol in his wash bag. As per normal, the names of the unfortunates on the radio did not register, but that was about to change.

"The death has occurred of Thomas Goy, Crosshill, Ballycroy, tragically. Removal this evening at…."

Sean did not hear the rest of the segment. He froze. His head throbbed. His heart began to pound like crazy. A feeling of despair and heartbreak came over him. He felt numb. A half-mouthful of soggy cornflakes remained inside his mouth as his tongue and cheekbones seized up. "This cannot be!" he thought to himself. As in Thomas's story, he tried to shout but nothing came out.

His mother was first to notice, as cornflakes and milk fell from the spoon that Sean was holding.
"Sean are you alright?!" she asked in alarm. There was no response, as she surveyed the frozen expression on her son's face. Milk began to cascade from his mouth.
"Peter come here QUICK!" she screamed at her husband and within seconds the newspaper was crumpled to the ground. And

so was Sean. His panicked parents did not know what was happening, and they screamed in desperation, thinking their beloved son was having a fit or a seizure that would threaten his life. Their screams alerted his sister who ran from the bathroom to join them.

Despite their scare, they were relieved to hear a noise coming from Sean after about a minute, to accompany his thumping of the kitchen tiles.
"NO! NO! NO!" he roared. Then he began to cry. Still hammering the floor with his closed fist as he lay belly down. His parents had never seen him do anything like this since he was a toddler.

Sean was oblivious to his parents cries of "What is it?!" and "Are you in pain?!" and "Shall we ring the doctor?!" as he tried to digest the news. The shock immediately brought back the dream that he had that night – a repeat of the previous night – when he had visualised a crying Thomas sitting at the end of his bed. An ice-cold feeling ran through Sean's spine. But he kept thumping and thumping repeating "NO! NO! NO!" His distraught family were in tears, they were so upset at seeing their loved one so upset. And they did not know what the reason was.

Mass was missed that day as Mr and Mrs McRobert and their daughter supported Sean. He managed to compose himself after about 15 minutes, to tell them that the lad who had given him a lift that Friday was just announced as being dead. Sean was embraced warmly by his upset but relieved family, all of whom were in tears.

In a broken voice, Sean explained that the 25 year old from Ballycroy had "everything to live for", "was great fun" and "was due to become engaged". He could not stop crying, as he recalled their laughing and singing less than two days earlier, when it seemed like they had not a care in the world. Now he was dead.

A phone call to an acquaintance from Ballycroy confirmed to Peter McRobert that it was indeed his son's new friend that was dead. He had been killed in a car accident just 20 minutes after leaving Sean at McGoldricks Bar. He had never made it home.

The confirmation of this news plunged Sean to new depths as his mind formulated images of Thomas's parents receiving word of his death. He recalled the face of the tall brunette who he had seen with Thomas in Dublin in The Big Tree Bar – who he assumed was Ursula - and imagined the heartbreak she must now be feeling. He tried to picture the wrecked Mercedes-Benz. And the unopened box containing the engagement ring. And the lifeless body of handsome Thomas.

Before long the GP Doctor O'Hare arrived, a close friend of the McRobert family, and administered some medication to calm Sean down. By 1pm he was asleep. Peter McRobert rang the parents of some of Sean's friends to say he was not feeling well and would not be returning to college that night. He also rang Yvonne's parents.

When Sean woke at 6pm he was groggy. His head ached as his mind tried to filter the news again. He could not believe he had lost five hours through sleep. When he picked up his wallet the card with Thomas's number fell from it. He sat on the edge of his bed and cried again. His sister came in from her bedroom and put a loving arm around him, and tried to console him.
"He was just so sound" sniffled Sean. "And there was this aura about him. Cool, confident, plenty of money, good job, talented – he even wrote songs. He even wrote a book too!"
"I am so sorry" she said. "But we are just so thankful that he did not crash the car when you were in it. Imagine what that would have done to Mum and Dad. Imagine what that would have done to ME! I love you so much!"
"He was everything I wanted to be!" cried Sean. "The poor lad. He never got to propose. He never got his house. It's so so so fecking wrong, Gracie!"
As Gracie led him to the sitting room where his parents anxiously waited, the song that was playing on her pink stereo as they passed her bedroom was – unbelievably – 'Never Let Me Down' by Depeche Mode! The song that Thomas had played just as he was leaving McGoldricks on Friday! Sean stopped and stared at

the stereo. He felt as if he was in a dream. "This can NOT be happening!" he said to himself as the lyrics embedded in his disturbed mind *"I'm taking a ride with my best friend. I hope he never lets me down again."* Was this God speaking to him? Taunting him – taking the mickey?!

Within seconds Sean had darted into the room and had kicked the little pink stereo against the wall, as Gracie howled for help. His parents came running and were astounded to see their normally quiet son smash whatever he could get his hands on – CDs, bottles of perfume, ornaments - as he flew into an uncontrollable rage. As his father tried to restrain him he lashed out at him, flattening him on the pink carpet as the women of the family screamed.

After a full ninety seconds of mayhem an exhausted Sean fled from the room. His bloodied father lay on the floor, checking his mouth. His mother and sister went to the man's assistance, both of them crying. His father was irate.
"He only fucking met the man on fucking Friday!" he roared. "You would swear he fucking knew him all of his fucking life!"
"Peter, please calm down, please please!" begged Joan. "It's the medication that did this!"
"Is it fuck!" he said. "Sure he lost the head this morning BEFORE any tablets! The fucker is gone mad. He must be on fucking drugs in Dublin or something! That's what he must be spending my fucking money on!"

It was a testing evening for the McRobert family as they tried to come to terms with the events of the day. Mrs Joan McRobert had never seen her son so disturbed. She had never seen her daughter so upset. She had never seen her husband so angry.

Sean came into the sitting room at 7pm and apologised to his father. He became upset at seeing his father's bruised eye and cut lip, and cried, before hugging him. Peter McRobert did not immediately embrace his son but did so once his wife beckoned him to. But another row flared up within minutes, as the family patriarch refused Sean's request to travel to the 'wake house' in Ballycroy before the coffin closed at 8pm:

"There's no fucking way I can make Ballycroy in an hour!" he roared. "And anyway, there's no fucking way I can show my face ANYWHERE looking like THIS!"

"Feck off so!" blasted Sean running from the house, leaving a horrified family behind.

"How will he fucking be when one of his REAL friends dies?!" asked the father, his eyes filled with tears. "I am afraid for that lad, I am telling you!"

Sean spent the next two hours crying at his grandfather's house. He rang his father at 10pm to apologise once more and say that he was staying with his grandfather that night. He also told him that Teeko was bringing him to the funeral Mass the next morning. His plan was to then get a bus back to Dublin on Monday evening. Peter McRobert agreed with his son's plans. For a second time he accepted an apology. He and his wife and daughter were now a bit more relaxed going to bed. They knew their son was in a safe place. But they were nonetheless still quite traumatised by the events that the day had brought.

For his part, Sean was hoping that a night away from his own bed might mean that Thomas would not appear in his dreams crying for a third night. But in a strange way, he wanted Thomas to appear to him. But not in an upset state.

As midnight approached, the hot whiskeys that Sean's grandfather had given him started to take effect, and the exhausted student fell asleep. The following day, he was going to bid farewell to the friend he had just met...

CHAPTER 9

Monday 7th October 1996

A legacy of Sean's grandmother's protracted illness leading up to her death some five years earlier was the bedside telephone in the room he woke up in that Monday morning. Indeed, his late grandmother was the person he dreamt about Sunday night as he slept in the bed in which she drew her final breath.

At 8am Sean rang Yvonne, who he knew would be getting herself ready for college. He spent several minutes explaining why he had taken the day off from his studies to attend the funeral of Thomas. As ever, his girlfriend was understanding:

"Of course you are doing the right thing Love" her refined accent travelled down the phone line. "I totally understand. It's almost poetic – as if you were chosen by God to accompany the guy on his final journey. And now you feel you must see the whole task through." This comforted Sean. She proceeded to assure him that she would be at Bus Arás bus terminal to greet him later that night, and that she would be spending the night comforting him in his bed. After the conversation came to a close, Sean shed some silent tears, as it struck him how much Yvonne loved him. A deluge followed as he was overcome by a feeling of immense regret for striking his father.

His grandfather interrupted by gently knocking on the door and entering the grey toned room. He told him that breakfast was ready, and that he needed to pull himself together as he had a testing day ahead. Sean's mother came to collect her son just before 9am, just after his grandfather had slipped him two £20 notes – one for petrol for Teeko and one for the bus fare that evening. The student gratefully accepted.

Back at home, Sean's mother had a suitable outfit prepared. A charcoal jacket, black shirt, brown pants and black polished shoes. He hugged her warmly, and apologised again for his behaviour the day before.

Just as he finished getting dressed, his father appeared at his bedroom door. His black eye and burst lip brought a gasp from the perpetrator.

"Oh Dad I am SO sorry!" he meekly mumbled, before his eyes began welling up again.

"It's OK Sean" was the reply, as the Castlebar man strode over and sat on the edge of the bed by his son. "I am worried about you Sean. PLEASE tell me if you are taking anything!"

"I swear I'm not!" said Sean, his head bowed as he wiped his eyes with a handkerchief. "It's just...it's just that it's SO unfair. It REALLY is Dad. I know I hardly knew him but I feel as if I did. And he was SO cool and SO successful. He wrote books; and songs...he had a good job...a nice phone, a nice car...a girlfriend he wanted to marry and a house he wanted to buy. He had travelled to SO many places. And he was SO happy."

"I know, Sean" came the reply. "But these things happen. It was meant to be. Our Lord obviously wants him back. And we hear of accidents every day. That's why I keep nagging you and Gracie to be ALWAYS careful. It's a cruel world out there."

Peter McRobert threw his strong right arm across his son's shoulder and neck and pulled him closer.

"I would have gone today with you but I can't – not looking like this!" he said.

"I'm so sorry Dad – I honestly don't know what came over me" replied Sean.

"You were upset. That's all. I realise now that other than your two grandmothers you haven't really lost anyone close until now. And – believe it or not – you ARE lucky, being nearly 21 and all! It was a big blow for you. But that's life. Sad stories like this happen ALL the time. We must try and brace ourselves for these things, and even then they are still as painful as hell when they come along. And life IS unfair. I agree one hundred per cent, Sean. I mean – you see young people dying in accidents and old codgers living to 100. You see fellows like the Rolling Stones and Status Quo taking nothing but drink and drugs and they survive – when young athletes and parents and teetotallers and non-smokers and vegetarians die! I mean, it's CRAZY! But life goes on. It HAS to! And after the burial today, just try and forget about the poor lad and get back to normal, alright?"

"I'll try Dad!" sobbed Sean.

"Come on now, Teeko will be here soon, and you don't want him to see you like this" said the father. "And here, give this £20 note to Teeko for petrol. And here are two fifties for the week." Sean gratefully pocketed the cash!

At 10am the glowing Opel Manta revved up outside of the Castlebar bungalow.
"My God, young Murphy" bellowed Peter McRobert as the impressively dressed Sean walked from the house to the passenger seat, "Isn't that car a bit too bright for a funeral?! Could your father not lend you one of those lovely black Audis of his?!"
"Ha ha Mister McRobert" grinned the bald headed Teeko. "This will dazzle them all in Ballycroy! You will be hearing reports of a UFO!" and off he spun, leaving the smell of burning rubber behind him.

Teeko was the friend that Sean had known the longest – since their first day in play-school. Christened as Sean Murphy, it became clear that one of the friends would eventually have to adopt another name, and the son of the garage proprietor was lumbered with the nickname 'Teeko' when he returned from a childhood holiday from abroad saying that he had been bitten by a 'Mostiqo'! His mispronunciation of 'mosquito' was to signal a life-long propensity to entertain family and friends with unintended malapropisms. Like when he told the lads that the 'parademics' tried to revive a dying man in an ambulance. And another time, when he was trying to describe how his soccer team made a last ditch bid to score an equaliser in a match, the unfortunate phrase that came from his mouth instead was "last bitch did"! A fun loving individual, the 20 year old had inherited the tendency of that strand of the Murphy clan for the males to go bald prematurely. So he had resorted to shaving his head instead. He was known to have a short temper too, but was popular amongst his male friends in particular, mainly due to his inherited love of anything that contained an engine.

The neatly nestled town of Newport marked the approximate one-third mark of their 48 kilometre trip north to Ballycroy. By the time the duo reached the banks of the beautiful Black Oak River, which looked like a river of flowing Guinness, Teeko had already heard too much about Thomas Goy, and was beginning to regret agreeing to transport his childhood friend to the funeral. He had little choice but to listen and concentrate on the road as Sean spoke incessantly about the man he had only met for three hours. As they passed the seven arches of the Newport railway bridge to their left, Teeko got to have his say:

"I'm getting mixed messages here, Sean, if you don't mind me saying so. On one hand you are saying he was 'sound' and 'talented' with his computer stuff and song stuff and all that. But yet you say he was a vindictive bollix, who held a grudge. AND he sounds like a racist. AND he sounds like a two-timer!"

"But THAT'S IT!" responded an animated Sean. "He was complex. Talented and contradicted. But he came from nowhere – a small farm in Mayo – to become a success in everything he did. Songs, computers, sport, women, travel...EVERYTHING he touched turned to gold..."

Except the fucking wall he crashed into!" Teeko quipped. "And so that's the end of him. Finito. It happens on Irish roads nearly EVERY day."

"But he made me feel lazy" added Sean. "He made me feel as if I have wasted my life. That I am only cruising through and doing normal boring things. He made me feel that there is so much more I could be doing with my life.

"Listen here..." said Teeko, in a serious tone as his car exited Newport on the grey overcast day. "If I did not know you any better I'd say you fecking fancied the man!"

"What?!" raged Sean.

"I mean it. After today, you better stop going on about him or the lads will begin to talk. Blokes don't glorify blokes like that. Footballers or singers perhaps, but not blokes who pick you up and give you a lift and tell you a few good jokes. I'm telling you as a friend. Just leave it after today, alright?!"

"You're bloody wrong Teeko!" came the response. "You would be the same if someone shared their hopes and dreams with you one day, and died just 20 minutes later!"

"That's where we differ!" replied Teeko. "No proper bloke shares his hopes and dreams with another bloke. Not in a car anyway. Maybe in a pub – after a dozen pints – but not in a damned car!"

Silence took over for the next several minutes. Sean was NOT impressed. He bit his lip and gazed out of his window, ruefully comparing the joy of his last long car journey with this one.
Teeko put on some more of his trance music, and started tapping his fingers on the steering wheel to the beat.
"It's 11 o'clock Mass – yea?" he asked his passenger.
"Yea!" sulked Sean.
"We've plenty of time yet so!" Teeko replied.
"Remember, I want to stop at the accident scene, it's just past Rosturk Castle. We just passed Nevins Bar and it's supposed to be a mile north of there. Oh. There is the castle out there on the edge, it must be near here, just down the road here I'd say, start slowing."

About a dozen bouquets of flowers marked the spot where Friday evening's crash had occurred. Teeko pulled his car into the right hand side of the road where there was a small space to park alongside a stone-built shed. The two men walked across the road until the flowers were at their feet.

"The poor lad" shuddered Sean, composing himself like his father had suggested.
"It's tough. No doubt about that" replied Teeko. "Loads of flowers here from women – perhaps he had more than two on the go!" Sean decided not to engage on that point.
"And it's a fairly straight stretch of road" he observed, looking at the stone walls that stretched either side of the flowers, in the shade of overhanging trees. "It's hard to know where he actually made impact. Maybe they rebuilt the wall since he hit the fecking thing."
"Come on, this is just too weird!" urged Teeko, pacing across the quiet road. "He's starting to get to me!"
Sean followed a few seconds later, solemnly.
"It's hard to believe it all ended there for him" he whispered. He bit his tongue from there as he knew he would get little sympathy from Teeko, who within seconds had the music blaring again.
Once more, Sean negatively compared his Castlebar friend to Thomas, recalling to himself how Thomas had always turned the stereo volume down whenever either of them wanted to speak that Friday afternoon.

By 10.45am the Castlebar youths had reached the peaceful churchyard in the middle of Ballycroy. Surrounded by a neatly crafted stone fence which had tall imposing oak and ash trees just inside its border, the cross-shaped church was attracting many mourners. The duo walked past the black hearse at the entrance to the aisle, and managed to find two sitting spaces in the second last row of the quickly-filling church. Sean took several deep breaths as he settled into what would be his seat for the next hour of his life. He knew that it would be an hour that would test him...

CHAPTER 10

Even before the Mass commenced, there was much sniffling from the top rows of the aisle, where the shell-shocked relatives of the 25 year old had congregated. Teeko surveyed the stained glass windows and pictures of the Stations of the Cross, almost oblivious to the air of sadness that was palpable to Sean. Sean could only see the back of the heads of those at the top row. He tried to deduce the mother, father and brother of Thomas. He guessed that the tall brown haired girl whom he could only see from behind was Ursula, and that it was her father who was literally providing a shoulder to cry on. The church was packed to capacity some ten minutes before the priest and servers appeared at the altar: and from the echo of voices Sean could tell that there were many who had to remain outside. At least the rain had held off for them, although the sky was still very grey.

As he took more deep breaths, his composure was tested by a friendly hand passing into his palm a Mass booklet. It was a single sheet, typed on both sides, with prayers on the inner side and a picture of a beaming Thomas on the front. Sean at once recognised the mischievous eyes, straight long nose, happy smile and parted long hairstyle. Sean felt like he had just received a thump in the chest. He fought back his tears as he remembered the laughing face from Friday. Now he was lying there, in a pine box covered by wreaths, lifeless. Just yards away.

He nudged his mate beside him and showed him the picture, which had the following words printed as a caption: 'Thomas Ivan Goy – 1971 to 1996 – Our beloved son, brother and friend.'
Teeko had a closer look at the picture before leaning up and whispering into Sean's ear:
"He's the image of your man from 'Bring Them Back Alive'! The Scarecrow, isn't it?"
All Sean could do in reply was to smile to himself. Typical Teeko! He had just saved Sean from crying! Teeko leant against his friend one more time for a second whisper:
"Did you know, in real life, yer man is married to Laura English Wilder!" Sean smiled again, before returning a whisper:
"Keep an eye out – maybe she is here in the church! And it's Laura INGALLS Wilder by the way!"

The back of the leaflet had a small message from the "heart broken Goy family" thanking the community for their support in the past few days. The quote on the bottom of the page came from a hymn and read "Be Not Afraid, I Go Before You Always". Sean smiled again. He was finding the funeral service experience as heart-warming so far. "Maybe" he thought to himself, "Thomas would have preferred 'Don't just get even – get ahead'!" And at that Sean scanned the crowd, wondering if the Mister Busybody on whom Thomas had exacted revenge was present.

The priest progressed through the Mass and thanked locals and strangers alike for turning out in large numbers, to be with Thomas's family in their saddest hour. When he mentioned the name of his girlfriend everyone could hear the cries of Ursula as she broke down again on the shoulder of her father. Many others wept throughout the church, as the priest himself took deep breaths to continue his homily. Sean strained his neck and his ears as he anxiously waited to hear more about the man he barely knew.

"Tommy Boy" said the priest "Was a nickname bestowed on this spirited young man, who was confirmed in this very church. Even that special day, I could see how impish and fun-loving he was. Many of you here were at the receiving end of his practical jokes, but we all know he meant no harm.

Thomas was a loyal and loving son, brother and boyfriend. A friend to behold. There was always entertainment when he was around. He tantalised us with his skills as a young footballer and bodhrán player, not fulfilling his potential in either before fluttering off to try his hand at something new and exciting – computers and travel for example. He was never boring, that's for sure, and life was never boring when Thomas was around."

Sean gulped as he recalled the words from the song 'Being Boring' by The Pet Shop Boys that jumped out from the stereo just three days earlier.

"And wasn't it like a stake through our hearts on Friday evening last when we heard the awful news of the accident in Tiernaur, which quenched the flame of this young man's life. Our prayers and love are with his devastated family, who we must support in whatever way we can in this - their hour of darkness. But as the words on the back of the sheet you have says – he now 'goes before us' – and he will be waiting there to greet us when our own day of reckoning comes. Until then, we in this plain-living parish of Ballycroy, have to dig deep within ourselves to find the strength to cope without one who we loved so much. One who we watched grow from a boy into a man. One who travelled the world and fitted into a quarter of a century what many of us could only dream of accomplishing in a lifetime."

Many in the church cried openly. It was clear to Teeko that Sean had indeed acquainted a special person, a much loved person. He began to feel a bit more sympathy for his friend.

Sean was proud that he had lasted this far without sobbing, although his eyes were teary. He even thought he glimpsed a tear in Teeko's eye. The spine-etching tones of the tenor from the brilliant Ballycroy Choir captivated all present, as the words of the hymn 'Abide with Me' travelled through the church.

Near the end of the service, the priest invited Gordon onto the altar. Gordon, tall with spiked ginger hair, was also 25, and had known Thomas since they were toddlers. They had gone to primary and secondary school together. He had a few words to say about Thomas. And as he stumbled through the opening paragraphs of his shaking script it was clear that the lad was very nervous. His initial attempt at humour failed miserably, which did not help his confidence at all. He should have known that saying he could picture Thomas speaking from his coffin that "I am dead, but GORDON'S ALIVE!" would be lost on the older members of his audience, and anyone other than those interested in 'Flash Gordon' and other science fiction films!

Eventually, the lad gained control of his breathing and touchingly recalled how Thomas had always strove to defend Ballycroy and anyone he believed was being treated unfairly.
"We were often taunted by those from other parishes that we were 'Bog-Men' but Thomas was always the first man to jump to the

front of the line and fight back. He always sided with the weak, with the underdog. He defended those being bullied. He was always quick to help a friend in trouble."

As he continued his eulogy, the Castlebar lads noticed that more and more people in the church were becoming visibly moved. Sean felt a hard lump in his own throat, but thankfully Gordon reverted to humour from his perch on the altar, and his anecdotes turned tears of sadness into tears of laughter – momentarily at least.

"I remember when the Bishop came to our national school when we were doing our First Holy Communion and asked where the Pope lived. Thomas put his hand up. The Bishop nodded his head and Thomas answered: "Pope-A New Guinea!" To Gordon's relief, everyone laughed this time.
"I remember his answer to a question one night at a local quiz, when we were asked "What is the only state in the world with a zero birth rate?" The answer is 'The Vatican' – but Thomas answered: "The Virgin Islands!" Everyone in the church – bar the priest and the organist – laughed.

"We remember the practical jokes he played, and the way he smiled when he caught someone out. Of course, he was not always around to face the consequences – like the time he used to steal whiskey from his father's cabinet, and replace it with Cidona so that it would not be noticed. That was, until visitors to the Goy household had to embarrassingly reveal that they were supping apple juice from a Paddy Power bottle!" That raised laughter also. Gordon was 'on a roll' now!

"And his friends from work told me yesterday evening that he used to spend so much time holidaying, that he was known to invite friends to his house to show them snaps of his office!" There was also a hearty response to that. Even from Teeko!

"His humour got us through many a long day at secondary school in Belmullet. Like when the Biology Teacher asked us what the initials D.N.A. stood for and he replied "National Dyslexic

Association!" There was suppressed laughter among the congregation to that.

"But my final and favourite story relates to when four of us spent a wintry night camping on the island of Inishkea South. On a cold blustery November night! It was a result of a teenage dare. Each of us brought a one-man tent. Of course, after an hour or so of trying to get settled, three of us started 'taking in water' as the rain lashed down and we found out that our tents were substandard. But of course Thomas had the best tent. A luxury tent. Water proof, wind proof – the lot! And as each of the three of us struggled in the dark, the lashing rain and the storm - he was complaining from his well-secured tent that his was so warm that condensation was forming and dripping onto him from its ceiling! We next heard him start up his battery-operated radio, and drink from his flask, as we shivered outside! He started complaining that he was too warm, and that he had to kick his socks off! Then, his tent lit up and I can still see his silhouette as he began reading with a powerful miner's lamp that was strapped to his head, crunching a bag of Tayto! While we famished! Eventually, after about a full hour of suffering the full blast of the Atlantic elements to which we were exposed, the three of us mutinied and stormed into his cosy tent. Three of us were wet from the cold rain and Thomas was wet from the warm condensation! Eventually he allowed us to defrost ourselves by taking a swig from his hot water bottle!" That story got the best reception, and Sean and Teeko looked at each other with tears of laughter in their eyes.

However, Gordon's comedy show had to come to an end, and he broke down as he paid tribute to his wonderful friend. "Thomas" he croaked "You were with us all the way until now. You stood with us and made us what we are. From Junior Infants to the Leaving Cert, you inspired us and kept us strong. We hoped we would repay you by standing by you when you became a husband and a father, as we know you would have been wonderful at both. But for whatever reason, God has taken you much too soon. Leaving...leaving us all utterly heartbroken. You would have been famous; we know you would, if you had been given enough time. As a writer or a computer expert, you would have made your fortune. But...but it is us who are left with the fortune that is the trove of happy memories you leave behind. We...we...we love you. We miss you. We are proud of you. We are proud that it was us you lived among. Proud that you are one of us. And we take...we take solace in this...this dark day...in knowing that your friendly warm smile will be there to greet us when God calls in the rest of us. May...may you Rest in Peace, Tommy Boy."

The sobbing friend received a generous round of applause as the undertaker and his staff moved to prepare the coffin for removal, and the smell of incense filled the church. Sean could see that everyone in the congregation was crying. Including Teeko, who bowed his head – but the tears falling on his shoes betrayed him. Gordon's speech had affected everyone. And it was clear that the popular young man was leaving a major void in the lives of the people from the area. The grief was tangible.

Sean got a close look at the grieving family members as they filed out of the church behind the coffin. The mournful moans that came from Thomas's mother pierced every sad soul present. Sean recognised the tall brunette from the day he saw her in The Big Tree pub – she was obviously Ursula. However, there was no sign of the stunning blonde from The Portobello Bar. He struggled to contain himself as he looked hard at the coffin, and imagined Thomas lying inside. "What a waste" he whispered to himself, as Teeko wiped a tear from his eye beside him.

The song that the Goy family had chosen to play to accompany the coffin's poignant passage down the aisle towards the church exit was Lou Reed's 'Perfect Day'. It was played on the public address system at a high volume so that it was audible above the wave of wailing sounds that swept through the congregation. Sean absorbed the lyrics and was struck by how appropriate they were for the few Friday hours he spent with Thomas:
"It's such a Perfect Day,
I'm glad I spent it with you,
Such a Perfect Day,
You just keep me Hanging On, You just keep me Hanging On."

CHAPTER 11

Outside the church, a light rain had started to fall. As the hundreds of mourners, predominantly dressed in black, spilled out into the churchyard to mingle with those who could not get in, an elderly voice came from beside Sean:

"The ould people used to say that 'happy is the soul on whose coffin rain falls' y'know!" Sean smiled and nodded, thinking it was ironic that it was a man in his seventies or eighties who spoke these words.

"Where are ya from, did you know Thomas?" he enquired.

"Castlebar. I did alright" said Sean as members of the local football team began to carry the coffin to the hillside graveyard just three hundred yards away.

"'Tis an awful loss to the parish, a young man like that" added the elderly gentleman, Sean studying his craggy weather-beaten features and the grey tufts of hair that peeped out from under his flat cap.

"It must be" replied Sean politely, as Teeko listened in.

By now the mourners were lining behind the coffin for the final part of the journey, with a silent guard of honour by local school children lining the route. The elderly man seemed intent on continuing his conversation with the 'strangers':

"Did ye see him within in the coffin?" he asked.

"No. We couldn't make it last night I'm afraid" replied Sean politely, thinking of Yvonne's earlier words that he was doing the right thing by accompanying Thomas on his final few yards.

"'Twas a strange thing. Hardly a mark on him. Bar the birthmark on his forehead – where the stone went through. Never saw the likes of it in me life!" said the old Ballycroy man. Sean felt his blood run cold, as Teeko strained his prominent ears in the rain to make sure he didn't miss anything.

"What do you mean – 'the stone'?" asked Sean.

"They say that when his car hit the wall, it barely made an impact on the wall and just slid along the wall 'til it stopped. There was hardly a mark on the car, save for a scrape all along the left wing and a hole in the windscreen, just one hole, you would swear it was a bullet hole! The guards said they never saw anything like it! Whatever happened the poor lad, he was unfortunate to hit a spot on the wall that must've had a loose stone on it, and the impact put the stone flying through the windscreen and right through his skull, just above the left eye where his birthmark was, 'Tis very strange! Never heard anything like it! 'Tis like the lad was marked for that ending!"

Sean struggled to find words. Teeko intervened to keep the conversation from being a monologue:
"So, it was kind of like the birthmark being a target?" he enquired. "I suppose you could say that" replied the old man as Sean felt his knees weaken. "Very odd. God must have branded him within in the womb, so he must!"

To a stunned Sean, the burial was like a haze after that, as he tried to digest what the old man had said. He felt his blood grow colder and took no notice of the ever increasing rainfall. Sean recalled the gripping story of the ghost of the little girl who had tried to take over Thomas. Had she finally succeeded? Had she targeted his birthmark – a possible 'weak spot' of some kind? Had the devil laid claim to him by marking him or something?

Sean was too shocked to say anything to the grieving families or the other mourners. It was up to Teeko to interact with some of the curious locals, and explain why they were there. A couple of them confirmed the story that a loose stone on the wall was supposed to have been fatal. Furthermore, they confirmed that Thomas was alive when someone came upon his accident. His eyes were open and he was trying to speak, but he could not be comprehended. Blood flowed from his entry wound, and the stone had lodged in the back of his skull. There was a theory that he may have been there for about ten minutes before anyone stopped to help him, as to some passing motorists it appeared that it was simply a driver who had pulled-in and stopped by the wall, such was the lack of apparent damage.

All of this news numbed Sean. He was mad at himself, as he should have prepared himself for the details. But he had not. By the time he and Teeko arrived into the orange car from the graveyard, the driver was fuming:
"What sort of man are you?!" he roared at the pale passenger. "I take the morning off work and drive you all the fucking way down

here to the funeral of someone I haven't ever fucking met – and it is ME who has to do the fucking empathising! ME! And YOU, you all upset and sad and everything, YOU didn't even empathise with his family or girlfriend. I had to! What sort of idiot are you?! And me soaked as well! And nearly out of petrol!"

Sean noted the anger, but hardly any of the words registered. He didn't even notice that his friend had said 'empathised' instead of 'sympathised'. As Teeko revved up the car and left marks on the churchyard tarmac, Sean was picturing in his mind the blood flowing from the birthmark. He was picturing the hole in the windscreen. He was picturing the dying Thomas trying to speak but being unable to. He was wondering what tune was playing on the radio. What Thomas must have been thinking. What pain he must have been in. How awful it must have been to have cars pass by for ten minutes and none stop to come to his aid. Sean shuddered as he thought of the agonising death Thomas must have suffered. He had assumed that the crash would have caused an instant death instead of a lingering lonesome one.

Even when Teeko blared his music as they swerved around the bendy road leading to the scenic coastal village of Mulranny, Sean was still deep in silent thought. He almost felt paralysed. He felt so empty. So sad. So annoyed that HE wasn't there to help Thomas in his hour of desperate need. Sean was in a type of trance. He took no notice when Teeko stopped for petrol in Mulranny – and paid for it himself.

It was only when they neared the site of the crash that the two engaged in conversation again:
"Jaysus, hard to believe he died like that" said Teeko. "And he sounded like one hell of a gas bloke. Your man the ginger dude was some comedian, wasn't he?"
"He was" replied Sean quietly. "Teeko, I'm sorry about the graveyard. I just went into a bit of a daze. I will contact his family again, I will write to them or something. I WILL. I just could not face them. Anyway, they were probably in a daze too. And I'm really grateful for you bringing me down, I really am. Dad still won't let me drive his car."

"It's alright" said Teeko as they approached the accident scene. "And I'm sorry for roaring, but I was all wet and everything. I was just annoyed. And I'm sorry too. I understand what happened to you. Jaysus look, looks like there's even more flowers there now!"
"It seems that way, doesn't it!" replied Sean as the orange car slowed down as they passed the bouquets on the way back to Castlebar.
"At least your man, the mental patient has gone" said Teeko.

Sean did not know what his driver meant.
"What did you say?" he asked, after pausing for several seconds.
"I said that at least your man who was there on our way down has gone. He must be gone back. They must have come for him. To bring him back to the synagogue - or 'the asylum' I meant to say."
"What man? Who are you talking about?" asked Sean.
"Your man who was there sitting on the wall when we stopped earlier on our way to the funeral, he was just down from us. You know the man. He looked like a mental patient. Out on day release. The man who I said was freaking me out and getting to me!" said Teeko, getting slightly agitated.
"I didn't see ANY man! There was no one there! And you didn't say anything about someone freaking you out!" asserted Sean.
"I DID say it! And clearly" said Teeko raising his voice. "I said 'he is getting to me'. Don't you remember?"
"I thought you were talking about Thomas – that his death was getting to you!" responded Sean, his mouth beginning to feel dry.
"And what man are you talking about. There was NO one there other than me and you!"
"There WAS! I swear to God. He was sitting on the wall just thirty feet away from us and the flowers!" insisted Teeko.
"Sure I would have seen him!" said Sean, now beginning to privately doubt himself.
"I thought you DID! Sure how could you miss him. He was sitting there on the stone wall, smiling at us, feet dangling, all scraggly like a geriatric patient, and holding a teddy bear!"

The words hit Sean like a train. He felt winded. Like he had just been punched in the gut. And he felt the hairs stand on his head and all down the back of his body.

"STOP! Stop the fecking car!" he roared reaching for the door handle.

"What the FUCK is wrong NOW?!" yelled a startled Teeko as he veered his car left into a grassy verge. Even before his beloved car ground to a halt, Sean had the passenger door held open and was vomiting the contents of his grandfather's breakfast.

"Don't ruin my fucking car! Vomit outside! Vomit outside!" shouted Teeko as Sean puked violently. "What the fuck is wrong with you, McRobert?!"

After several minutes of cursing to himself, Teeko got out of the car and went to the aid of his friend, who was now out of the car on the grass on his knees. He had emptied his stomach, and had no more to expel. He was pale. He was sweaty. He looked like he was 50 years old.

Teeko reluctantly hauled Sean up by grabbing his arms. They both stumbled to a nearby galvanised gate that led to an emerald field and leant on it as cars sped by. It was raining steadily. Sean was shivering. He spat into the field a number of times. He was hyperventilating. He looked into the eyes of his friend, and managed to speak:

"Tell me. No messing now" he panted. "You DEFINITELY saw a man holding a teddy bear at the site of the crash?!"

"Of course I did! How could you not see him?! He was there as clear as that black heifer over there. And he had a teddy bear held on his lap!" replied Teeko with conviction.

"Fecking hell!" replied Sean, still shivering AND sweating.

"Look at you!" said Teeko. "You look like you have seen a ghost!"

"The thing is..." panted Sean in return. "...It is YOU who has just seen a ghost!"

CHAPTER 12

Tuesday 8th October 1996

Sean woke up in his Castlebar bedroom. His weary eyes gazed at the ceiling. He tried to remember what day it was. He went to look to his left to see what time was showing on his digital alarm clock and that's when the aching activated. He had a horrendous hangover. He could feel his brain throb inside of his skull. He crushed his eyes shut and gritted his teeth. It was 8am. And Tuesday. He was now into his second day of missing lectures.

As he struggled out of his bed, he felt as if his brain was bouncing from side to side inside his skull. Every move caused him agony. His mouth was parched, he needed water. 'Cardboard mouth' was the term one of his friends used to describe that dehydrated hangover feeling. As he began to slowly dress himself, images from the previous day began to re-surface in his mangled mind.

Images of him and Teeko 'on the session' knocking back double brandies in a Newport bar in the middle of the afternoon. Images of him care-freely spending the cash that his father and grandfather had given him.

Then the images gradually became more disturbing. The 'friendly' barman wiping blood from his bloody nose. A massive man in uniform restraining him. "A Garda! Oh no!" Being bundled into a car. Being roared at by his furious father! "Oh no, this is getting worse!!"

Within an hour of making his appearance in the family kitchen, both of his parents had scornfully reminded the hungover youth what he had done the day before. The images were not dreamt-up ones, they were real! The awful throbbing in his head grew faster and louder. He began recalling Monday afternoon's events:

After realising that he had just seen a ghost, Teeko had insisted that he had to stop off at the nearest bar for some alcohol to "calm me nerves!" Of course, one quick set of double brandies led to another, then another, then another – before the vodkas started to arrive across the counter. Of course, the friendly barman obliged every request and was glad to accept the notes from Sean's wallet. But when the notes ran out, he respectfully refused the drunken demands for credit. Furthermore, when the barman realised that the bald-headed half of the duo had a car parked outside and intended to drive it home, he came from behind the bar and tried to convince him to part with his car-keys. The ensuing argument progressed to the main street of Newport, and the cold October air accelerated the effects of the alcohol and made Teeko more aggressive, ending with him head-butting the barman!

A Garda happened to be on patrol nearby and he ran to the scene, which now saw the assaulted barman punching Teeko AND Sean. Luckily, as the Garda was intervening, Sean's uncle, the vet, was driving through Newport and he pulled up his car and tried to assist the policeman in restoring order. 'Luckily' because he convinced the Garda that he would bring the twosome home to Castlebar in his jeep, and the bleeding barman – content that his nose wasn't broken – swayed his head when the Garda asked if he wanted to have the two men taken to the station. The poor barman just wanted to see the back of the drunkards. Back in Castlebar, the parents of both rounded off their day with the proverbial tongue-lashing they deserved. Then it was time to enter a state of post-spirits stupor!

Mister Peter McRobert was still angry on Tuesday morning, and had no mercy for the physical suffering of his son Sean:
"You have the family SHAMED! I could hardly look my brother in the eye last night!! What the HELL is wrong with you?! Drinking and fighting in Newport! I will never be able to show my face in that town again! And spending all of my money! Well, I'm telling you this – you'll get no more! NO MORE I say! Back up to Dublin now with you today and don't come back here until you cop yourself on – do you hear me??!!"
"Ah please, calm down" intervened his upset wife.
"CALM DOWN?! CALM DOWN?! I AM CALM!!" roared the McRobert patriarch. "He should be getting a boot in the behind! And talking about ghosts and all of that rubbish. The only spirits he saw were in a glass!!"

The tirade continued as Sean sat by the kitchen table and tried to study the bus timetable. He knew his mother would replenish his wallet for the week. He knew his father would eventually cease his yelling. But for now, he just wanted to get rid of the headache, and so he asked his mother for some tablets.

"Tablets!" his father yelled. "You must be taking plenty of tablets and pills, you! Losing the run of yourself over someone dying - someone you barely met! Dublin must have turned you into a druggie, young man! A ghost! And ye didn't even have the brains to realise that the ghost who ye were supposed to see came from a novel – from a book that was made up! Fiction - not a REAL story at all! You have made FOOLS of us ALL!" And with a final warning to his son to stay in Dublin until he was "sorted out" he stormed out of the house.

Sean decided he would be fit enough to endure the 12 noon bus back to Dublin. After getting some money from his mother, he returned to his room to prepare his rucksack. As he rummaged through his clothes and toiletries he wished he had a mobile phone so that he could check-in on Teeko to see if he was receiving similar punishment. He wondered how Teeko would collect the car from Newport and bring it back. All of this distraction was finally shunting aside thoughts of Thomas Goy.

But as Sean stood up and shook-down the navy Mayo GAA jacket, he noticed something fall from it onto the floor. Still reeling from the effects of the alcohol, he gingerly knelt down on the carpet and checked what it was. It was a navy box. About the size of a matchbox, but thicker. Made of velvety material. It looked like a jewellery box. "Where did that come from?" He gently opened it. And staring up at him was a glowing diamond solitaire ring. "Fecking hell!" he exclaimed. "How did that get there? It must have come from the jacket...but...?"

Sean reached for the jacket with his left hand and stood up, still holding the box and ring in his right palm. He then left them on the bed cover. He shook the navy jacket again. Then he realised – it wasn't his! There were no red and green stripes on the shoulder, it was ALL navy except for the Mayo GAA crest. Then he checked the size – it was XL whereas his was just L. This was the WRONG jacket!

He eased himself onto a sitting position on the edge of the bed and rummaged through the jacket as his hands began to shake and he began to perspire. Through the mire that was the hangover in his mind, the reality hit him that the jacket he was now holding belonged to the man whose burial he had attended the day previously. "But...but that means... that means that HE has MY jacket!! I must have taken the wrong one with me as I was leaving the car!! My father is right – I AM an idiot. I AM losing it!"

His theory was confirmed when a small maroon diary fell into his palm from an inside pocket. The front of the diary had the name 'Thomas Goy' neatly scrawled, with his Dublin address and phone number listed beneath. Sean's hands trembled even more. Again, he felt a cold feeling run up his vertebrae. He was holding the diary of a dead man. And he had his engagement ring there on the bed. "This can NOT be true!"

His thoughts were disrupted by his mother calling from the kitchen to say they had to leave shortly so that he could catch the bus. Sean managed to roar back and say he was on his way. He rolled the jacket up and put it into the top of his bag. He zipped the diary and the diamond into a pocket in his pants. His mind was in a twirl, but he had what he needed – and he would have a four hour bus journey to digest the latest development.

Yvonne had left a message with his mother to say she would call to see him that night. But Yvonne was not foremost in Sean's thoughts. Neither was his mother. Thomas Goy had regained 'pole position'. As the Bus Eireann coach roared out of the county of Mayo towards the east coast of Ireland, Sean, sitting alone in the back seat, carefully studied the stunning diamond. It was beautiful. How Ursula would have loved that. He wondered what he should do with it. He felt so giddy with excitement. Even dead, Thomas was generating thrills for him. What a man!

Sean was keeping this information to himself for now. The giddiness was helping him forget his hangover. He thumbed through the little diary. His hands still shook. He noticed names, numbers, addresses, little reminders, and tots of figures. He wasn't yet able to focus on every page – but he would do so once he calmed down. He felt close to Thomas. He looked up at the twenty or so fellow passengers in front of him and wondered what was going through their mundane minds. "If only they knew what I just found" he grinned to himself. But there was another surprise in store from beyond the grave:

Upon re-checking Thomas's jacket to see if it contained anything else, Sean felt something bulky within it. He put his hand as far as he could into each of the three pockets but his flesh could not lie on the object. He hoped it was a wallet. He began to tremble again as he tried to figure out what it was and how he could get it out. It was inside the lining of the jacket arm, the left arm, high up towards the shoulder. After a few more seconds, Sean finally figured it out. What he thought was a string to tighten the jacket was actually a shoelace that had been attached to an interior button. He tugged on the shoelace until it drew its prey towards a small opening in the inside stitching. Sean felt like a fisherman, and he could not wait to see what was at the end of his 'line'. Soon, there it was. The opposite end of the lace was knotted to a leather pouch. Sean's eyes threatened to bulge from his head as his heartbeat thundered in anticipation.

He finally managed to control his fingers so that they revealed the contents of the leather pouch. It was CASH! LOADS of CASH! ALL fifty pound notes. He had never handled such a wad of money before. As his heart pounded his chest he tried to count it. "This must be the house money!" he thought to himself as he recalled that his ill-fated friend had mentioned putting a deposit on a house. "A diamond, a diary and dosh!" he thought to himself. "What a day! What a fucking day!"

Sean's face beamed all the way into Dublin as he contemplated what he would do. "Sure no-one other than Thomas will know about this – it's all MINE!" He felt like shouting aloud to tell everyone his good news, to share his joy. But bottling up all of his excitement was fuelling his new-found energy and zest. The hangover had evaporated – along with his money worries. His latest count of the cash was coming up with six thousand pounds! He was struggling to contain the happiness he felt within himself. The thought of handing what he had just found back to the Goy family had briefly entered his thinking, but was banished almost as quickly as it had arrived. "This was MEANT to be! This is FATE!" he convinced himself. "To HELL with my father who laughed at me – I don't need him or his money NOW!"

The coach from Mayo arrived in Dublin's Bus Arás city centre terminal just after 4pm. Sweet svelte Yvonne, dressed in her usual 'arty' style of a long flowery patterned dress, was bewildered when the passenger she had come to meet was in a much brighter mood than she had expected. She had programmed herself into 'sympathy mode' to help her boyfriend get over the trauma of the fatal car crash and its collateral damage. She had planned to treat him to a romantic night to help get his mind to a happier place. But he was ALREADY in as happy a place as she had ever seen him. He was radiating happiness! She could not reconcile his smiling face with the phone calls from Mayo that weekend.

But that happiness was not to last...

CHAPTER 13

Wednesday 9th October 1996

"My God are you OK Sean?!" asked Yvonne in her dulcet Dubliner tones to her perspiring boyfriend at 2am in the morning as she sat up in the bed beside him.

"What the fuck is going on in there, will ye shut-up to fuck!" roared an annoyed student voice from the corridor.

"I'm sorry…I'm sorry…" panted Sean. "It's just…just a nightmare I had!"

"You poor thing, you were screaming" whispered Yvonne, gently wiping sweat from the side of his face with a towel.

"Jaysus, it was so fucking real!" Sean continued. "SO fucking real. It was scary!"

"You poor thing, you are drenched!" repeated Yvonne. "Go for a shower for yourself".

"I'd better not, sounds like I woke the lads already, they won't be happy!" replied Sean, breathing a little more easily.

"Was it him you dreamt about, Love?" asked the Dubliner.

"Yea. But it's alright, I'm OK now, let's go back to sleep, sorry for waking you Yvonne", said Sean.

But although he had just dreamt about Thomas, he was continuing his recent trend of divulging very little. He had given Yvonne the impression that it was just a nightmare about the crash, but it was more than that. And as she switched off the bedside lamp he was glad that he was not alone in that bedroom.

The nightmare he had just experienced had brought an angry Thomas to Castlebar golf-course, demanding that Sean return what he had found in the jacket that day. In the scene, the dishevelled looking car-crash victim, with blood pouring from his head wound and birthmark, had stormed on to the 18th green in front of all of their combined families. The incident had embarrassed Sean in front of everyone. Thomas was foaming from the mouth in anger, and threatening to "destroy" Sean. "I won't just get even, I will get ahead!" the angry Thomas had snarled. "Just give me back my belongings or you will pay!"

As Yvonne drifted back to sleep, her lover was unable to. He was afraid to sleep. But as threatening as the dream was, it didn't diminish his resolve to hold onto the money and the ring. He was already making plans for that windfall. And he was getting a thrill out of the fact that he was keeping all of this to himself. Only HE knew. He would not even tell his girlfriend; in case word somehow wriggled its way back to Ballycroy that there was jewellery and cash to be claimed. He could not take the chance that Yvonne might convince him to give everything back. This was just TOO exciting.

Sean thought hard and deep to himself as the dark hours passed. "This is not like me!" he admitted, recalling that he had never stolen anything and had been brought up by his parents to be a good Catholic. But what had all of that goodness yielded? What had he gained from it? All he had to show was a life of boredom, a dull, colourless life. Now he was dazzled by the sparkle from the diamond. The sweet smell of the fifty pound notes filled his senses with all sorts of possibilities. He was on a high. In three hours, Thomas Goy had pumped more adrenaline into his veins than twenty years had. Sean felt that his brain was now FULLY functioning, that it was TOTALLY active, and not at all the run-of-the-mill under-utilised nucleus it had been. Even in the darkness, his mind seemed more alive to all types of possibilities. It was as if the blinkers had been removed – he could now see a lot more. He stroked the long locks of auburn hair of the sleeping Yvonne. Already she was becoming a victim of the new sweeping change that was occurring in Sean. Up until the previous week, the touch of her soft skin meant everything to him. He yearned for no other. But now...now it was different. He would be more like Thomas Goy – she would be just ONE of his women. "With this treasure, I can choose my pleasure!" he thought to himself, as the morning drew closer. "Thomas Goy – what a guy!"

That afternoon, Sean sat in the Cathal Brugha Street lecture theatre with his fellow Environmental Health students. But as most of them listened attentively to their lecture and jotted notes, the 20 year old Mayo man was day dreaming. Boredom had caused his mind to wander. He was thinking of how he would spend his money – which now totalled eight thousand pounds as he had cashed-in the diamond ring in a city centre pawnbrokers that morning. He had to try hard to keep himself from smiling constantly. His mind was racing with all kinds of exciting plans. He had NEVER felt so good in his life. He had purposely chosen to sit away from Yvonne in class that afternoon, as it gave him a chance to look down at the small diary that he opened on his lap. It measured only about 6 inches by 4 inches, so it was easily concealed. It was divided into alphabetical sections. His eyes scanned the names scrawled on it – mostly female. He wondered who they were. He was particularly interested in finding out who the petit blonde he had seen accompany Thomas in The Portobello Bar was. Was she Debbie Willis? Or Charlotte McNab? Or even Jacqueline O'Kelly? Maybe Thomas had not even listed her in his little maroon book.

As the lecture concluded, Sean was satisfied with his plans for the evening. To Yvonne's disappointment, he told her that he would not be able to join her for coffee and that he planned to spend the evening catching up on the lecture notes he missed on Monday and Tuesday. He slipped off in the direction of O'Connell Street where he hailed a passing taxi and gave him the address in Ranelagh that he had memorised from the diary. He was on his way to see Norman – the house mate that Thomas had mentioned on Friday.

As he opened the gate that brought him onto the pathway to the semi detached two-storey house, he noticed a navy 1984 registered Volvo parked down the leafy avenue. He guessed that it must have been Thomas's car. He took a few deep breaths as he approached the door. He then calmly took a stick of chewing gum from his pocket and placed it on his tongue as he pressed the doorbell. Through the glass on the door he could see a tall figure approaching. The door was opened by who he assumed must be Norman.
"Yes, can I help you?" asked the tall thin man.
"Are you Norman?" replied Sean, trying not to focus too much on the enormous forehead and receding brown curly hair of the man standing by the opened door.
"Yes, why?" came the stern reply.
"I'm Sean, a friend of Thomas's...."

"Oh Jesus come in, come in!" urged the tall man in his Kerry accent. "Jesus, I only heard the news an hour ago. I'm still in shock so I am...I did not expect you so quickly!"

"You are expecting me?!" enquired Sean in a surprised tone.

"Yes, yes – his mother mentioned that one of his friends would call to collect his stuff, but I did not expect you so soon. Sit down, sit down. Is it Sean, did you say? Jesus, Jesus I'm still in shock!"

"So you just heard today?" asked Sean, sitting into the cold leather chair in the untidy sitting-room.

"Just an hour ago – his poor mother rang" replied the Kerryman. "She was apologising for not contacting me sooner. No one thought to contact ME. It's awful, awful so it is. I can't believe it. I mean – Thomas – DEAD? How can that be? Dead and buried before I knew it?! Jesus, I have to get down to his grave!"

Sean spoke in calm tones as he tried to get Norman to slow down. He found the Kerry accent hard to understand at the best of times, never mind when a Kerry person was rushing his words. As he studied the state that Norman was in, his mind was working overtime on how best to capitalise on the situation. But Norman was making it easy for him:

"So, you are a cousin of Thomas's, yes?"

"Yes" lied Sean without blinking.

"His mother mentioned ye might come for his stuff" repeated the disorientated Kerryman. "His room should be open. Jesus, I can't believe it. He's DEAD! Were you at the funeral? Of course you were, why am I even asking? I'm none the better of this shock. Will you have a Jameson with me? Or a can of Tennants?"

"No thanks" replied Sean. "Sure, I'd better take the Volvo with me. I won't risk a drink in case the guards are pulling. Can you show me where his room is and I'll make a start? Are you sure you are OK, Norman?"

"I'm still in shock, I suppose" answered Norman. "He's dead and buried ALREADY?! I can't blame his poor family, they had enough on their plate, but I cannot believe I was sitting on my arse here all weekend watching shite on the telly when my house-mate was being waked down in Mayo! I just CAN'T believe it. Sorry – I forget your name again – John, is it?"

"John, that's right!" replied Sean with a smirk.

73

"John, let me show you his room. Give me a shout if I can help. Jesus, I don't know though if I can go in there and go through his stuff. It's just too unreal!" muttered Norman.

"I'm still in a daze myself" said Sean calmly. "Hard to believe we won't be seeing him again. He was so full of life. And did his mother tell you that there was barely a scratch on him?"

"How do you mean?" asked Norman.

"He barely hit the wall, just skidded alongside it, and a sharp stone that was loose on top of the wall shot through the windscreen and pierced him!"

"Jesus No!" answered Norman. "The poor fella. The poor fella. I will have to leave this house. I cannot live here anymore now. Poor Thomas. He never knew on Friday that he was leaving here for the final time. Isn't it awful, John, isn't it?"

Sean left Norman to fix himself some alcohol in the kitchen while he had a look around the room that Thomas used to live in. He gazed at the undressed bed. At the awful light blue walls. At the yellow flowery curtains. At the boxes of documents under the window. At the slippers, towels, socks and underwear strewn on the floor. At the grey television set in the corner. At the bottles of aftershave and cans of deodorant on the bedside locker. At the shirts hanging in the creamy wardrobe. At the set of spare keys dangling from a hook on the wall. At the books, CDs, video cassettes and audio tapes in a box in the corner. In the midst of all this, a sparkling black Hi-Fi system stood out. It even had a remote control!

For a moment, Sean pictured what the Bruce Boxleitner lookalike must have looked like laying back on the bed, with the blonde babe by his side. He wondered how many women must have accompanied his hero to this very room. He wondered what Thomas's thoughts must have been as he packed his bags on Friday morning. "Little did he think at McGoldricks that I would be the next person to step into his room, the poor bloke" he sighed to himself.

But Sean had work to do. By the time he was back in his rented Drumcondra bedroom that evening, he had it adorned with the new Hi-Fi system. And he had just trebled his CD collection! As

74

the beat from the song 'Behind the Wheel' by Depeche Mode belted through his bedroom as midnight approached, the student peered out of his window at 'his' Volvo which he could see beneath the street light below. "I will surely get a grand for that!" he smirked to himself, "But first I will need to unload everything from the boot into here in the morning. More lectures missed – but what the heck! Tomorrow will be another fun-filled day!"

CHAPTER 14

Thursday 10th October 1996

Yvonne was becoming increasingly worried about her boyfriend. There was no sign of him at lectures or tutorials. Or even in the canteen. It was a rainy morning so she thought that might have been his excuse for not attending college.

The lashing rain had not deterred Sean from leaving his student accommodation. By 10.30am he had unloaded all of Thomas's boxes from the Volvo. By 11am he was sitting in Ladbrokes Bookmakers on Dorset Street, gambling some of the cash he had received for the diamond. But he wasn't just there to gamble, he was on the lookout for a familiar face – the ragged face of a Dublin man known as 'Chucky'.

Chucky was a grey haired, flat-nosed fifty year old north-sider with whom he had become acquainted with when gambling. At first, he had been a source of annoyance to Sean and his fellow students as he always had bad B.O. and drooled from the mouth. But after some time, his astute knowledge of horses had meant that his 'tips' had helped Sean and other young gamblers multiply some of their county council student grant money!

An overt sympathiser to the Irish republican cause, the Dubliner had earned his nickname from his regular phrase 'Tiocfaidh ar lá' pronounced 'Chucky-or-Law' which was borrowed from the Provisional IRA motto, translating as 'Our Day Will Come'. His anti-British ramblings had made their impact on the impressionable young men, but seasoned north-siders knew that he was full of bluff. 'Real' IRA activists would always be much more discrete and would not be drawing attention to themselves. Nevertheless, Chucky had acquaintances who were involved in the IRA, and he had many links in the Dublin underworld.

When he arrived into the bookmakers shop just before midday he had a greeting for "Young Seanie from May-O" before he went to check the runners and riders.
"On the doss again?" he laughed, "Wasting the tax they scrounge off of me!"

"You never paid a penny tax in your life Chucky!" shouted one of the regulars, as Sean made his way over to him.

They stepped outside and had a 'business conversation'. Several minutes later they were shaking their hands beside the blue Volvo.
"Agreed. One thousand pounds for me, and you can keep whatever extra the scrapyard give you for it" said Sean.
"Deadly, Seanie!" drooled Chucky, knowing he had already made his morning profitable. "I will be back in ten bells with the dosh, and then yous can leave it to me. And yous don't be worrying that culchie head of yours, no one will ever find out where the car came from – or where it ends up!"

By 1pm Sean had an extra thousand pounds in his pocket. His heart was thumping. He was on such a high. He had never dreamed he could have so much money. The priorities that had existed prior to that week – his family, his education, his girlfriend – were now falling well down the pecking order as cash and goods took over. The Castlebar man had a new habit to feed – greed! And the possible consequences were not even featuring in his new selfish thoughts.

That afternoon, he ignored the knocks on the door as he sat in his rented bedroom, going through the belongings of the late Thomas. He knew the person knocking on the door was Yvonne, he could just not be bothered entertaining her. He had too much to do. Books, diaries, albums – this new treasure chest was going to take some time to catalogue. As regards lectures, he had already decided to 'write off' the week. The knocking eventually stopped and he peeped out of his window to see Yvonne's pink umbrella head back down the road. He didn't care that she had walked over an hour in the rain to see him. He didn't care that she would have willingly satisfied the lust for flesh he was experiencing. He knew that his feelings for her had all but evaporated, but if he was to break it off with her it would just complicate college life. She was highly thought of and popular amongst the student body, and he knew that anything that was seen to hurt her would create too many irksome enemies for himself. It was better to keep the relationship going for the moment anyway.

Feeling hungry that evening, he brought the maroon diary with him to 'Some Like It Hot', his favourite kebab shop. While he waited for his order, he carried out his plan and entered a nearby phone box with about two pounds in coins. He opened up the diary as the rain pelted against the glass. There was a Dublin number listed under the name 'Jacqueline O'Kelly'. He nervously dialled the number. It was like someone else was guiding him to do this. He knew what he was doing was wrong, but boy it was exciting! His mouth began to feel dry, and he thought of the Coca-Cola he would have in five minutes. After a few seconds of ringing, a female Dublin accent answered the phone:
"Hello"
"Hello, is this Jacqueline?" asked Sean
"It is. Who's calling?" she replied.
"Sorry. You don't know me. My name is Sean. I am a friend of Thomas Goy."
"Thomas Goy? And why are you ringing ME? Did HE give you my bleedin' number?" she asked crossly.
"No, no – it's not like that at all!" answered Sean. "Please let me explain..."
"This better be bleedin' good!" she curtly replied.
"I'm sorry to ring you like this, but Thomas was talking about you last week..."
"He WAS?! And what was he bleedin' saying, the bugger?!" she shouted.
"Sorry. Sorry Jacqueline. Just please listen" begged Sean. "He was praising you. Talking highly of you..."
"And how did yous get my bleedin' number?!" interrupted Jacqueline.
"Please listen. Just give me a chance to explain! Please Jacqueline..."
"OK so, go on!" she replied, taking a deep breath.
"I found your name and number written down. Just this afternoon" continued Sean. "I found it amongst some of his stuff. You see...the thing is...Thomas died in a crash last Friday night. He's gone."
There was silence at the other end of the phone.

"Jacqueline, are you there?" asked Sean. The silence continued for about ten seconds as Sean put another coin into the slot.
"I don't believe it, you're joking me?" she said, barely audible.
"I wish it were true, but he is dead" replied Sean.

The Dublin girl mumbled a few things and the Mayoman could not really make out what she was saying, but he did not want to waste any more coins on her and decided that he would capitalise on the shocked Jacqueline by tantalising her:
"Sorry Jacqueline, I have to go here, sorry" he said in a rushed voice.
"Don't go yet!" she begged. All of a sudden the tables were turned. She now wanted to keep Sean on the line.
"What was he saying about me? Yous HAVE to tell me. Don't leave me like this, PLEASE! Please Sean!"
"Listen, I have to go! I will give you a call; same time tomorrow night, OK?"
"Oh please don't go. What happened him? What did he say about me? PLEASE?" she implored.
"I will talk more tomorrow night. I PROMISE! Bye Jacqueline" said Sean before hanging up, leaving the desperate girl at the end of the line.

As he tucked into his oily kebab, Sean smiled into the distance. He felt like a cat toying with a mouse. He was in charge. He was going to make this Jacqueline BEG to meet him. He was going to feed her a load of rubbish. Tell her what she wanted to hear. And get what he wanted to get.

After finishing his kebab, he entered the same telephone box and rang Yvonne. He apologised for not meeting her and said he was just worn out. She accepted his apology and excuse, and urged him to have an early night. She offered to meet him and stay with him on Friday night but he said that he just needed some space to clear his head. He lied that he was still having nightmares and did not want to ruin her sleep. Of course, all he was doing was clearing a path for further dishonesty.

Later that evening, as more music from Thomas's CD collection blared, Sean went through a pile of paperwork from one of the boxes he had taken from Ranelagh. There were three pleasant surprises for the thief. First of all, he found the envelope marked 'Die in Ohio'. Inside, an old receipt for ten thousand dollars from Cyber Music Inc., along with a sheet with the typed lyrics, signed by Thomas.

His second surprise was a bound script for the ghost story Thomas has mentioned. It was marked with a hand-written 'final draft' and soon enough Sean found that the bulk of the paperwork in that box was formed from earlier drafts. He could not wait to read the story – entitled 'The Mayo Ghost Story'. But as he prepared to start reading, the third surprise came into his hands – to round off another exciting day since the arrival of Thomas into his life. An unmarked white envelope at the bottom of the box yielded two thousand dollars in cash!

Sean shrieked with joy, and rose up to punch the air. "Yessssss!" he roared above the music. "This just keeps getting better and better! Thank YOU Thomas Goy! Thank fucking YOU!"

Nine thousand pounds in Irish currency and two thousand dollars lay under the mattress of Sean McRobert as he smiled himself to sleep that night. And the nocturnal dreams brought him happy images of him and his Ballycroy buddy driving along Route 66 in the USA in an open-topped Cadillac, with cash coming from the exhaust pipes as they spun towards a golden sunset, joking, laughing and listening to loud music, their fringes blowing back in the wind. Both in dreams and in real life, a week had changed Sean's life in a way that he could never have imagined....

Die in Ohio

I Want to Die in Ohio,
And not in this Mire,
I Want to Die in Ohio,
By my Family Fire.

I Want to Die in Ohio,
Among her Green Hills,
I Want to Die in Ohio,
Before my Blood Spills.

I Want to Die in Ohio,
When this War Ends,
I Want to Die in Ohio,
Surrounded by Friends.

I Want to Die in Ohio,
And not in Vietnam,
I Want to Die in Ohio,
And be buried with Mam.

God Let me Die in Ohio,
So that when I am Dead,
You will Get Even with Satan,
And then Get Ahead.

CHAPTER 15

Friday 11th October 1996

Sean woke with a smile on his face. And it wasn't the thought of the bundles of cash that lay beneath him. He was simply recalling a quote that Thomas had mentioned almost one week earlier on their sole journey. It was a quote from the tennis player Vitas Gerulaitis, who, having just beaten Jimmy Connors for the first time ever after losing the previous 16 matches between them, said: "Now let that be a lesson to you all. NOBODY beats Vitas Gerulaitis 17 times in a row!"

Of course, when Sean had repeated that story to his mates on the Castlebar golf course he barely received a chuckle, which reinforced Sean's belief that he and Thomas were in some way 'soul mates' as they shared a similar outlook on life and in many ways a similar sense of humour. For a moment, his thoughts focused on the grieving Goy family and Ursula. How awful they must be feeling. He wondered if they had yet realised that most of Thomas's belongings were missing. He wondered if Ursula had realised that she had been just hours away from being an engaged woman. But, these thoughts dissipated as Sean turned his attention to Friday evening. He had a fish wiggling at the end of the line and he would have to reel her in!

The 'fish' of course was Jacqueline O'Kelly who anxiously waited by her telephone as 6pm approached. The day had passed so slowly for her, as she paced through her cosy Rialto bedsit. She was not able to concentrate on her research work. She had so many questions to ask Sean. But the day was passing quickly for Sean. He had spent most of it shopping, treating himself with 'his' cash. He splashed out on expensive shoes, trousers, belts, boxer shorts, shirts and a leather jacket in Dublin's city centre. To top it off, he bought a bottle of cologne that cost one-hundred pounds. The shop assistant joked that the scent that came from it was cash!

Of course, Sean purposely left it until well after six o'clock before he dialled Jacqueline's number. Unlike the previous night, she barely let the phone ring once before she breathlessly answered it:

82

"Hello, is this YOU Sean?"

"It is Jacqueline, sorry I'm late but I got held up" he lied.

"That's fine, that's fine" she panted. "Now, tell me exactly what Thomas said please."

"Listen Jacqueline, I was thinking, perhaps it would be better if you and I met face to face. What do you think?" asked Sean, disconcerting her.

"Well...perhaps...well..."

"How about later this evening, I'll bring you out for a meal!" asserted Sean.

"Really?! But...I don't know...maybe..."

"Listen. I'll pick you up in a cab. Just tell me where to pick you up!" he said confidently.

"Jaysus, I don't know..." she replied clumsily.

"You don't know where you live!" laughed Sean. "Now Jacqueline, come on!"

"Sure I don't know yous!" she replied.

"Well. You knew Thomas too so at least we have a starting point" he said.

"Maybe. OK so. Tonight so, yeah? Are you sure?" she asked.

"I'm giving up my Friday night for you Ms O'Kelly. My pleasure. Thomas would have approved. Actually, it was just this time last week the accident happened...."

"Where did it happen, Sean?"

"Near his home in Mayo" he replied. "Listen, I will tell you all about it later. Now, just name a time and place and you will be picked up – AND brought safely home again" said Sean, admitting even to himself that it felt like he had just received a combined injection of charm and confidence.

The couple proceeded to make their arrangements. There was nervous excitement in both of their bedrooms as new clothes were tried out in front of mirrors. Sean was fitting a strange woman into the most hectic week of his life; Jacqueline was fitting a stranger into what had been the most boring week of her life – up until Sean's phone call. Sean wondered if the woman he was about to bring to dinner was the sexy blonde that he had seen with Thomas in The Portobello Bar. He hoped it was.

83

As arranged, at 8pm the taxi beeped its car horn outside of her Rialto bedsit. The fine-smelling Mayo man sat in the back of the cab, his leather jacket shining under the streetlights, his hair gelled back. He caught his first glimpse of the researcher as she paced in her high heels towards the vehicle. She was NOT the blonde. She had curly long hair and looked nervous. She was medium height and very slim. She wore a long black coat but as she entered the back seat it opened to reveal a black dress and black patterned tights. She smiled at the glowing Sean, who sat behind the driver.

"Excuse my manners, I should have got out and opened the door for you!" were his first words.
"It's alright" came the Dublin accent. "Sure it's NOT a date, just a meeting, right?"
"Right!" asserted Sean. "Now. Your meeting tonight is in Tanta Zoe's restaurant in Temple Bar – is that alright with you?"
"It sure IS!" said Jacqueline, relieved that Sean looked 'normal' and someone she immediately felt comfortable with.

In the taxi, Sean filled-in his captivated companion on the story of Thomas's final hours. Tears came to her eyes as she imagined how dreadful his death must have been. And she could not cope with the thought of the lively man she knew now lying dead six feet beneath the surface. By the time she sat at the table of the Cajun restaurant she was feeling extremely emotional.
"So. What did he say about me?" she asked, her teary eyes reflecting the candlelight of the sparsely attended eatery.
"Well. On at least two of our previous car journeys together he mentioned 'Jacqueline' to me" said Sean. "And I always noted a particular glint in his eye when he mentioned your name!"
"Really? You're joking me?" she said, her narrow face brightening up.
"For sure! No messing!" laughed Sean. "I asked him how serious you two were but he always just smiled and looked totally ga-ga!"
"Get away!" she replied.
"No seriously. He did. That's why I had to call you when I came across your number. I was hoping you might already know..."

"No, I didn't know at all! And I am so upset that I missed the funeral and did not get a chance to kiss him goodbye..." she said, before breaking down in tears.

"Here" said Sean, handing the vulnerable girl a new handkerchief. "Well, I hope you get some consolation in knowing that you were the last girl he ever spoke to me about – you were obviously high in his thoughts – and as I was the last person he had a conversation with I guess that means you were the last girl he EVER mentioned!" lied the manipulative Mayoman, as Jacqueline gulped back her red wine to try and calm herself.

"So, how did you two meet?" asked Sean just after the waitress took away the remnants of the main course. "Thomas never quite got to fill me in. As I said, he always became distracted once 'Jacqueline' entered the conversation."

"We just met by chance, one night last year in GiGi's Night Club, and he just charmed the knickers off me, the rogue!" said Jacqueline, her head beginning to sway as the effects of the red wine kicked in. Sean sipped his slowly. He was purposely keeping sober as he wanted to take full advantage of this lady. He wanted to watch her melt in front of him, and then be powerless as he moved in to have his wicked way.

"So...so Sean" she stuttered as they downed dessert. "So what EXACTLY did Thomas say about me last Friday night?"

"Well Jacqueline" teased Sean, "Being a gentleman, and you being a lady, perhaps I should not say..."

"Oh will yous go on and tell me and stop the bleedin' messin'!" she slurred noisily, as the handful of other diners looked around.

"OK, OK – just keep your voice down!" said an embarrassed Sean. "Well...er...well...he said that you were his 'Rialto Rodeo Girl'!" whispered Sean across the table of the dimly lit room.

"Ha ha!" she laughed loudly, swigging back more wine. "The randy bugger. His 'Rialto Rodeo Ride' more like. Oh, he was something else. That's typical him!"

"Typical him is right!" smiled Sean, happy that his gamble was paying off.

Several hours later, the scheming student was still smiling. And he had plenty of reasons. The sight of Jacqueline's tights and dress on the carpet of her bedroom. The sound of her snoring from behind his naked body as he lay beneath her blankets. The heat that came from her shapely but intoxicated body.

He had just two-timed the lovely Yvonne. And it felt great. Not one iota of guilt. This was THE life. Thomas had served him up 'a slapper on a platter'. He quickly dressed himself and escaped from Jacqueline's bedsit before she woke up. He would never phone her again. He had got what he had wanted. Any more contact would bring unwanted diversions and waste wanted energy. She had nothing on him – where he 'worked', where he lived, what his surname was. He was just 'Sean from Mayo'. "No address, no telephone number – no bother!" As he paced towards the city centre from Rialto, he could not wait to get back to the diary and try his luck with another phone number...

CHAPTER 16

Saturday 12th October 1996

It was well past midday when Sean rose from his slumber. The exertions from his night with Jacqueline had tired him out. He looked at his new clothes hanging in his wardrobe. He smiled as he thought of all of the money that he was lying on.

As the rain pelted against his bedroom window, he wondered what might be happening in Ballycroy. Were the Goy family still too busy grieving to realise that he had pulled a fast one on Norman? Had a real family member turned up at Norman's to claim Thomas's belongings? Would anyone remember him and Teeko from the graveyard?

Next, he thought of Castlebar. How was his mother keeping? How was his sister Gracie? Had his father calmed down? Had his bruises healed? Was his grandfather alright? Were the lads out golfing again?

After assessing his eventful week, Sean promised himself that he would try and attend college EVERY day for the coming week. He would put in an almighty effort, even though his interest in the topic of environmental health had greatly waned. He thought about Yvonne. He had neglected her all week. It was time to make some kind of amends – even though deep down he knew that he was rapidly falling out of love with her. Just a week earlier there was no way that he would have even contemplated looking at another woman – never mind sleeping with one.

But his fresh experience with Jacqueline had whetted his appetite. It had caused a power surge within him. He could not believe how easy he had conned her. And now he was thirsty for more.

However, later that day, from a different phone box – Sean had received a different type of reaction when he phoned the girl listed as Charlotte McNab in Thomas's diary. It quickly became clear during their phone call that this was a streetwise chick. She insisted on meeting him in a public place. Of her choice. And a time was agreed – 12 noon on Sunday at The Square Shopping Centre. Again, Sean was hoping that she was the blonde from The Portobello Bar.

After taking stock of the cross-channel football results in the evening, Sean took a taxi to Clontarf where he met his girlfriend Yvonne at her parents' house. He had got the taxi driver to drop him off some distance from the house, so as to give the impression he had caught a bus. He did not want Yvonne or her parents to question how a student could afford taxi fares.

She was delighted to see him, and her parents made him feel as welcome as ever. He took pride in the fact that he was able to simply 'park' his indiscretion from the night before, and act without the slightest hint of guilt. He apologised for not spending more time with her that week, and declared that he would not miss a minute of college for the coming week. The couple spent two hours enjoying each other's company before Sean made his way back to Drumcondra.

He treated himself to two quick pints in Quinn's busy bar before making his way to his accommodation. He grew excited as he anticipated his meeting with Charlotte the following day. But he knew that she sounded like a challenge, he would have his work cut out to bed her.

That night, he fell asleep in much the same manner that he had done since 4th October – recalling his trip with Thomas. He hummed some of the tunes that had blared from the stereo of the Mercedes-Benz. It felt as if that three hour segment was crystallized – that he could recall every second. As he hummed the tune of 'Being Boring' by the Pet Shop Boys he smiled – 'boring' was now something he could never be accused of being.

Sunday 13th October 1996

The newly-wealthy student continued to contribute to the profits of Dublin taxi drivers as he got one to transport him to The Square Shopping Centre in Tallaght. Again, he had spruced himself up and was dressed to impress in his new gear. He tried to remain as cool as he looked as Charlotte kept him waiting at the coffee shop she had nominated, at the base of the escalator. He looked around at the countless shoppers. He looked up at the levels above him and wondered if she was watching him. He sipped at the water he had bought himself as he wasn't a drinker of tea or coffee. She was over half an hour late....

Then, the vision appeared in front of him. It was HER – the blonde from The Portobello Bar. She too was wearing a leather jacket, but a smaller red one. She wore a black top and jeans, with red shoes. Her blonde hair was now curlier, and the smile she was wearing seemed somewhat forced as she approached him, clutching her handbag which hung over her right shoulder.
"Sean, is it?" she said reaching out her hand.
"Yes indeed, pleased to meet you Charlotte" he replied shaking her hand, which she drew back very quickly from him as she took a seat opposite him, her curly blonde head bowed. She looked fantastic, as attractive as he had remembered, but definitely much crosser!
"What will you have?" he offered.
"Oh just a black coffee" she replied. "I won't be staying long. And sorry I'm late..."
"Not a bother!" came the reply just before he placed an order with the waitress. He asked for another bottle of water as he felt his mouth drying up. He was in the presence of beauty and he tried not to stare at her luscious red lips and beautiful blue eyes. He wondered what he would say next but Charlotte took over:
"I don't know how you found out about me but I am NOT impressed and do NOT want to be here!"
"I'm just...." attempted Sean but it was clear that she was going to be a much more difficult prospect than Jacqueline.
"You're just WHAT?" she jumped. "Trying to capitalise on Thomas's death?"
"Oh...you knew already that he was dead...I was just letting you know in case you hadn't...."
"Oh I knew he was dead alright! I have my sources! And I don't need any weasel like you. I know your type!" she snarled, her pretty features contorting.
"You have me wrong – totally wrong" replied Sean. "I have better things to be doing with my Sunday; I just wanted to tell you that

Thomas had mentioned you in his final hours. I have nothing to gain. I am just a plain student who..."

"Who dresses up on a Sunday like he is going to a night-club? Who goes through the diaries of dead men?!" she growled as her coffee arrived.

"You have me wrong, I am telling you..." insisted the shell-shocked student.

"Well I am telling YOU that I am RIGHT, and that you are a liar! And I will tell you why. I know that Thomas would NEVER mention me. To anyone. Especially to a weasel like YOU! He had a girlfriend, and I have a boyfriend, and what we had was a secret. It was just sex and nothing else. The man is dead and I don't care! But I DO care about people trying to take advantage!" she said as Sean began to perspire. He was on a loser here and it was time to escape and minimize the damage. He could already feel the gaze of other customers as Charlotte's voice grew louder. He attempted to rise from his seat.

"SIT DOWN!" came the order from the petit blonde who was now morphing into a Rottweiler.

"Now. Don't you EVER contact me again!" she hissed. "I have a good mind to report you. You are lucky my man did not answer your phone call. You only had one intention and that was to feed me a sob story and get into my knickers. Now dream on! Only real men like Thomas get in there, and certainly not boys like you! You disgust me! I can see right through you!"

"Think...think what you like...I don't...I've done nothing wrong" stuttered Sean. "If you and Thomas were so secretive, how come you were in The Portobello Bar together?"

"What? So you were spying on us too, you little weasel! I don't believe you!" she snarled, growing angrier.

"I was NOT spying I was just drinking!" spat Sean, rising from his seat, and picking up his change. "I did my bit. Now I'm off. I'm sorry I bothered!"

"Fuck off you weasel!" hissed the blonde, who now had the attention of not just the fellow imbibers but the passers by. Sean disappeared into the crowd. He felt that his face was scarlet. He wiped sweat from his brow. "Wow" he thought to himself. "For such a pretty little thing she is pure rotten to the core. Beauty MUST be only skin deep!"

Sean was still smarting by the time he got back to his bedroom. He checked the diary for the third number he was going to ring. He decided that he would leave that for later on in the week. For now, he still had lots of Thomas's stuff to get through. He played another couple of his CDs – albums by Radiohead and The Divine Comedy – as he read through love letters from Ursula. The contents aroused him. If only Ursula had known about the other women that Thomas had in Dublin. Thomas's infidelity helped eradicate any feeling of guilt that Sean had about being unfaithful on Yvonne. But as he drifted off to sleep, he recalled the motto "Don't just get even – get ahead." What would Thomas have done if he had found out that Sean had 'hit-on' two of his women - and was about to 'try' a third?

CHAPTER 17

Monday 14th October 1996

Sean woke from his sleep. Something has startled him. He was feeling very cold. The quilt had fallen from his bed. He pulled it up and wrapped it around himself. He glanced at the digital radio that showed it was 2.13am. He buried his head deep into his pillow. He wanted to go straight back to sleep so that he would be fine and fresh for his morning lecture. He lay onto his back. He was still cold. He tried to sleep again. But he felt strange. It was like his skin had left his body and that his veins and bones were exposed. He had never felt like this before. He grew colder. He decided he would rise from the bed and try to get a warm jumper as otherwise he might catch a 'flu'. But when he went to rise he felt that he could not move. He went to move his legs but nothing happened. He tried the same with his arms, but again, no movement.

He wondered if he was having a stroke or something. He tried to say something to himself but it felt like his tongue had doubled in size and in weight within his mouth and he was unable to move it. Then he remembered the story that Thomas had told him about the spirit of the little girl trying to take over him. Is this what was now happening to him?!

He tried to look again at the digital clock on his bedside locker but by now his head and neck were paralysed. They were facing upwards towards the ceiling. Then, the terrified student began to feel as if he was levitating towards that ceiling. He felt as if his body was being lifted by some unseen force from his bed. Was he dying? Was this the end? He tried to shout for help but nothing came out. He tried to gulp but he felt that the saliva was drowning him. He could only breathe through his nostrils. He was totally helpless. He felt ice cold, the exact sensation that Thomas had described. That the blood within his veins had frozen solid. That every single hair on his body was standing upright and was white.

Then he felt it, the spirit of the girl. He could not see her, but he knew she was there in the room. Right beside him. To his left.

He tried to move his head to look at her but he couldn't. He could feel her presence. She was so close. He waited for her to touch him. Then, just like Thomas, he felt like his body was being taken over, from the toes up, inch by inch, slowly. It was as if the girl was squeezing the life out of him and replacing his body with her own. He could feel her desperate sadness. It was if her sadness was being transfused into him.

As the takeover of his body passed his privates towards his stomach, he expected to hear the door open by one of his housemates. As far as he was concerned, he was roaring at the top of his voice for help. It was a savage, mournful roar from deep within his soul – which was quickly being smothered by this young sorrowful girl. But of course, no one came to the door, because his roar was just an inner roar – no one could hear it.

As the alien force approached his chest he tried to gulp again but he couldn't. He was gasping for air, drowning, suffocating. He felt that once his mind was taken over that was IT – he would be dead. His body and soul would be hers. He recalled what Thomas had done when he too was in this paralysed state. And that was to pray. In his mind, he recited the rosary at a rapid pace. Simultaneously, he begged his late grandmother to come to his assistance and say the rosary with him. He felt her presence at the right side of his bed – and suddenly, the advance towards his neck stopped. The spirit felt angry. It felt annoyed. Sean could sense all of this. It was as if the little girl was saying "I was almost there, why didn't you let me finish!"

Very quickly, Sean felt the girl's spirit disappear. He was relieved to be able to clear his throat. He was able to move his limbs. He was so happy. But his grandmother, whose presence he had felt right beside him, warding off the evil takeover attempt, had gone too. But he felt her warmth still. She had come to his rescue. His body was no longer cold. He sat up in his bed, still frightened and feeling exhausted. He looked at his digital clock. It was STILL only 2.13am! To him, it had felt like he had just fought an eternity for his life. But the incident had just lasted seconds!

As hard as he tried, he could not sleep another wink. Although he had not seen the girl with his own eyes, or his grandmother, he knew that he had been visited by ghosts. They had been there. In that room. From the afterlife. He recalled what Thomas had said about having a new appreciation that there was another world out there. An alternative world that had to be respected. Sean had now experienced the return of the dead himself. And it was hard to fathom, difficult to describe. He had never thought it possible to feel so cold and to survive. He would never again take for granted what a gift it was to be able to move a finger and his tongue. Although he knew that Teeko had seen a ghost in his presence just a week earlier, it was only now that he could fully appreciate how frightening it was, to be so helpless in the presence of stronger invisible supernatural forces.

Instead of being in the lecture hall at 10am, Sean was fast asleep. He was now exhausted from the sleep interruption of the previous night. Daylight crept through the blinds in his room. In Cathal Brugha Street, Yvonne was annoyed that her boyfriend had not showed up. He had broken his promise.

When he awoke, Sean spent a couple of hours reading the script on the ghost story. It was clear that Thomas had effectively integrated his own scary experience into the script. It was a captivating story, and sent shivers down the spine of the student. Only the arrival of his angry girlfriend that evening was more frightening! She scolded him for not attending his Monday lectures and he promised that he would redeem himself for the rest of the week.

In fairness to him, he was true to his word and by the time the weekend arrived Yvonne was a much happier girl. She had spent a night in his bedroom, and their relationship seemed to be firmly back on track. But her seemingly devoted boyfriend had plans made for the weekend that would not involve Yvonne. The third and final girl's name in the diary was Debbie Willis. Her number would be the next to be rung. Sean made excuses to both his mother and his girlfriend outlining why he would not be in their company that weekend. Both women fell for his lies. But the weekend would bring its own troubles for the man who was still reeling from his encounter with the world of ghosts...

CHAPTER 18

Saturday 19th October 1996

Sean spent the early part of the day taking Thomas's boxes from their hiding place under his bed. He had to hide them – and the expensive music system – when Yvonne had visited as she would have asked too many questions. It was a bright but cold morning, and after reading through the ghost story script again he decided to wander into the city centre and buy himself some more new clothes. On the way, he stopped at his usual bookie shop on Dorset Street to see if there were any 'tips' from the regulars there.

"Any more motors for me, Seanie?" whispered Chucky into his ear as he studied the boards. The stench of alcohol from his breath made the Dubliner instantly recognisable.
"Not today, Chucky!" replied Sean, his eyes still scanning the information in front of him.
"I suppose you haven't a spare tenner to loan me?" asked Chucky. Sean obliged the grinning scoundrel.

Several minutes later, when still leaning on a ledge 'studying the form' on the newspaper cuttings in front of him, he felt the familiar coldness of the unwelcome spirit descend upon him. He tried to move his arms and legs so that he could stand up straight, but he was paralysed. "Oh no, not now, not here in front of everyone!" he thought to himself as he tried to look around at the other punters. But he could not budge a millimetre. Any of the rogue element present could have put their hands in his pockets and relieved him of the two hundred quid he was carrying, and he would not have been able to do a thing about it.

But losing money was the last thing on his mind, as he felt the spirit of the girl try to enter his body and mind. He was helpless. He could feel her beside him, lower down to his left. And then he felt her rise, and an even colder feeling came to the left side of his head, as if the ice queen herself was about to kiss his left ear. Again he began to pray. He tried to pray aloud, but nothing came out. Then, came a hissing sound right into his left ear. He thought his heart would stop. It was the scariest thing he had ever heard. A raspy, evil voice from the depths of hell. "Let me in!" were the words. "Let me in!", "Let me in there!" repeated the satanic voice. He felt like crying but like all other parts of his body, his tear ducts were frozen. He hoped Chucky would approach and perhaps frighten away the spirit. He wondered if any of the other gamblers had spotted that he had been struck into a statue.

The hellish tone that rang through his brain from his left ear was torturing him. "Let me in!", "Let me in – take me!" was now echoing inside his skull. He thought of his grandmother and prayed again. He tried to close his eyes but couldn't. They were transfixed on the list of horses named on the sheet in front of him. The name of the horse that captured his vision was 'Mary Beth'. But it was the desperate cries into his left ear that was thwarting his attempts to pray. His spirit tried desperately to fight off the evil presence that was ascending slowly but surely from his feet to his neck. He tried to focus on praying and the words 'Mary Beth' appeared to dance in front of his eyes.

"Lordship Lane, Uttoxeter, two-fifteen" were the next words into his ear, as the ghastly presence disappeared like a quenched candle. This time, the words came from Chucky. Sean shuddered as he realised that he had regained control of his senses and body. He was never so happy to get the stench from Chucky's breath! The intervention of the Dubliner had frightened the poltergeist away.

Sean had to compose himself by having a drink of brandy in Patrick Conway's pub. The spirit of the girl had made another attempt to take over him, and he was rattled. He wondered how she had made the connection between him and Thomas. The same ghost? Had she been in the Mercedes-Benz with them? Had she been at the funeral? Had she been the cause of Thomas's crash? He swallowed a second brandy and walked to Henry Street where he bought himself one of those new mobile phones. Next he went to Clerys to buy a new shirt and belt. He had a date to keep that evening.

Debbie Willis had not known of Thomas's death when she received the call earlier that week from Sean. She was genuinely shocked, and they had agreed to meet in The Stoneboat Bar in Kimmage that evening at 6pm. So that she would recognise him, Sean said that he would be sitting at the bar wearing his orange Baltimore Orioles baseball cap. And he would be drinking orange.

There was no taxi or bus transport involved for this *rendez-vous* as Sean was determined it would be more successful than his experience with Charlotte in The Square Shopping Centre. Despite his consumption of alcohol, he had hired a car for the evening. And not just any car – a Jaguar! The ultimate seduction aide!

As he sat at the counter of the quiet south-side bar, he wondered what this third lady from Thomas's diary would look like. She sounded quite refined on the phone, almost posh. He wondered what their connection had been. Perhaps she might have been just a solicitor or an accountant? But all of his contemplations did not factor one possibility – and the surprise he received almost floored him.

"Hello, you must be Sean" was Debbie's smiling greeting. For a second time that day, the Mayo student was dumbstruck. The tall, attractive woman who had just introduced herself – was black!

The images that cluttered Sean's mesmerised mind were of the irate Thomas gesticulating wildly at the African motorist in Enfield. And his racist tirade. "Surely" he thought to himself, "Thomas could not have been so two-faced?"
"Eh...eh...Hello. Hello Debbie!" he stuttered. "I am...I am indeed Sean, and am very pleased to meet you!" He was struck by her huge eyes and protruding red lips. She had short hair and looked stunning. She reminded him of Uhura from the Star Trek series, but she was even more of a beauty. He ordered her a drink and suggested that they sit at a table in the corner facing each other. He brought his fresh orange and her bottle of Harp Lager down from the bar. He removed his orange baseball cap as he was

beginning to feel warm, and he threw his leather jacket on a third chair.

The evening passed quicker than any evening that Sean had ever known. It was 10pm before he knew it. He was shocked. He was in love! Debbie Willis, daughter of a Zambian mother and an English father, was one of the most beautiful women he had ever laid eyes on. She worked as a fashion buyer for the retail chain BHS, and lived in nearby Harold's Cross. She had the most wonderful, sensual, soothing voice that melted him. She was intelligent, kind and humorous. The more the minutes passed, the more Yvonne became less and less important. He was now REALLY in love.

After a couple of lagers, Debbie revealed that she and Thomas had only had a couple of dates, but that nothing had come of it. Confirmation that she had not slept with Thomas came as music to Sean's ears. She was surprised that her name had even been in the diary, and – in complete contrast to 'The Square Psycho' – she said that Sean was "really thoughtful" to have contacted her.

The arrival of such an intelligent and invigorating 'date' caused Sean to change his course, and he told her that the Jaguar was just being minded by him for a friend that weekend. He hoped that Debbie would meet him again, and so he did not want to be lumbered with an ongoing rental bill! The Jaguar was designed for a one-night stand, and although the signs were that a lady like this would not 'oblige' on the first night, that there might be opportunities in the future.

She agreed to let the student link her arm to her home nearby just after 11pm. He pointed out the Jaguar as they passed it and received another "really thoughtful" plaudit! After about ten minutes, they found themselves outside of the house she shared with two other girls.
"Do you mind if I leave the 'inviting you in for coffee' part until the next night?" she asked. Sean thought his heart would jump from his chest.
"The next night?" was all he could muster.
"Well – if you WANT to. No pressure!" she replied alluringly.

"Of course. Of course. Definitely!" said Sean, instinctively reaching down to clasp her hand. "I'll ring you. Definitely!"
"I look forward to that" she smiled, the exterior light from the house shining on her like a theatrical spotlight.
"Can I kiss you?" he gulped. Debbie smiled. Then she approached him, put her hands on his shoulders and gently pulled his face to hers, and they shared a smouldering kiss on the doorstep.

Sean was in heaven! He felt as if he was floating back to the Jaguar. He was madly in love. "Thank you Thomas Goy!" he shouted as he revved up the car engine. The cost of the car hire meant nothing to him. That kiss meant more than any sexual encounter with any other woman could.

As he went off to sleep that night, it was the beauty of Debbie Willis that saturated his thoughts. But he was just a couple of hours away from another horrifying night visit from the spirit that he had now christened 'Mary Beth'. And for the next fortnight, she would attack him again several times, and each time the power of prayer eventually managed to ward her off. But she was persistent...

CHAPTER 19

Friday 1st November 1996

Sean tried to sleep as the crowded bus left the capital city. It was a mild winter's evening, and he flopped back on his seat and gazed at the charcoal sky as the bus headed westward. This would be his first visit home in a month. He had never been this length away from home. He was looking forward to seeing his mother and sister again, but not so much his father. He put the headphones of his new portable CD player into his ears and tried to find a comfortable position in his seat. There was a younger male student beside him, also bound for the West of Ireland, but Sean had little interest in conversing. He was jaded.

The last week had been stressful. It had seen him break off his relationship with the sweet and popular Yvonne. Although this move had given him the freedom he desired to fully focus on his budding relationship with Debbie, it pained him to see Yvonne's tears and the heartbreak he had inflicted on a girl he still cared for. The broken tones of her voice reverberated in his brain. He frowned as he recalled the cross faces of their class mates, especially the females, who had rallied around the ditched girl. And some of their cutting comments. A year ago, such a hostile reaction would have broken him. But now Sean McRobert was a steelier creature. He had developed a thick neck. "Sticks and stones may break my bones but words will never hurt me" he thought to himself, a quote he had found in one of Thomas's jotters. But even that was not true. The ghostly words that he had heard from 'Mary Beth' had indeed hurt him, and had caused him much sleeplessness, contributing to his overwhelming tiredness. In a peculiar way, he was becoming used to her 'visitations'. But he wanted them to stop. He hoped that the bus would not follow his bedroom, his bookies and his bathroom as her latest port of call.

To help ward her off, he was now wearing a blessed rosary beads as a neck chain. He found it had helped. But he would have to hide that from his parents – especially his father – as it would give them ammunition for their theory that he was "going off the rails." He would also have to hide his mobile phone, his new

101

expensive shoes, his broad-buckled belt, his new tattoo and his CD Discman as they would only invite unwanted queries into his wealth. He had continued to accept the weekly payments from his mother into his bank account, even though he had more than nine thousand pounds under his mattress. He had to – otherwise there would be questions. Questions he did not want to deal with.

As the coach sped through Leinster, Sean continued his struggle to get comfortable in the tight seating structure. "A far fecking cry from the Merc!" he thought ruefully to himself as he recalled the trip from exactly four weeks previously. A smile took over his face as he dug into his memories from that unforgettable evening. He closed his eyes and recalled the chats, Thomas's jokes and stories, the music, and the sing-songs. He re-pictured the extreme expressions on Thomas's face, from the laughter to the venomous racist outburst to the fearful look as he recalled the ghostly visits. He remembered how happy Thomas had looked as he left Castlebar that evening. Sean's eyes began to well up as he thought of how happy Thomas must have been – with a new wife and new home on the horizon – only to meet with the end of his life within the hour.

Sean wondered what song might have been playing as his car hit the stone fence. He wondered why he had lost concentration on a relatively safe road. He wondered if perhaps Thomas had reached back for his jacket only to find that he had Sean's jacket instead and that the ring and cash were gone. Maybe THAT was the cause? Or maybe Mary Beth had tried to take over him that evening? Or maybe the ghost of his great-grandfather with the teddy bear had appeared on the road and distracted him?

The words of 'Perfect Day' came back to the student and he focused on the line *"You made me forget myself; I thought I was someone else – someone good."*

Thinking about Thomas had become an obsession with Sean, and he was alert to this. He was simply fascinated with the man and the life he had led. His interest in his college course and his girlfriend had dissolved in that month. He knew that he had become changed by the money and females that resulted from meeting Thomas. Changed for the worse, perhaps, but in Sean's opinion being 'nice' and 'boring' had not gotten him very far. He wanted to be ruthless like Thomas was in exacting revenge on those whom he believed had wronged him. Sean knew that no one had 'wronged' him as such, but he wanted to chart a life for himself in which women, wine and wealth were predominant.

"Thomas's months-mind Mass is probably this weekend" he thought to himself, knowing that he could not show his face in case he drew attention to the missing car and belongings. He could memorise every word that was spoken at Thomas's funeral Mass. He was in awe. Sean wanted THAT life. He wanted to have a church full of crying people if he ever died. He wanted to have friends queuing up to quote anecdotes from his eventful life. He wanted to be admired. To be loved. And now – thanks to his illegally obtained means – he felt he had taken his first steps. He was now on the verge of having a sexy exciting girlfriend of means – instead of a student girlfriend. Within the past month, he had kissed three different women – almost as many as he had kissed in total in his life 'BT' – 'Before Thomas'!" He now had the respect of Chucky and other gamblers who had noticed him 'flashing the cash'. He had displayed a cruel streak to his fellow students by callously ditching Yvonne. He now had rebelled against his father – something that he had felt he needed to do. And through his drunken incident with the unfortunate Newport barman, he had experienced the thrill of getting on the wrong side of the law. Furthermore, the way he duped Thomas's housemate Norman, showed that he was 'a natural' at deception.

An exciting few weeks lay ahead, and Sean continued smiling as the busload of students from the west neared home. With Yvonne no longer a burden, he was free to progress things with Debbie. He had plenty of cash for gifts to woo her further. He would no longer have to hide Thomas's belongings as Yvonne would not be visiting his room any more. He was contemplating abandoning his degree course, as he had lost total interest, and now he was *persona non grata* amongst his fellow classmates. He was sure that he would be able to do something with the ghost story script and the songs that he had found in Thomas's box. But he needed more time to engineer his options.

At the same time that her ex was approaching his home town, Yvonne was pouring her heart out to an old friend Nadine in Toddy's Bar at The Gresham Hotel. Friends since childhood, Nadine had come from her studies in Belfast to offer support to her distraught friend. Yvonne tried to control her sobbing as she provided an update:

"He changed so much in the past month. Ever since that damned accident in Mayo. He became totally obsessed with that Thomas guy, he really did. He started letting his hair grow and parting it in the middle, just like him. He was always quoting his jokes and stuff that happened to him. You would swear he knew him for years – for goodness sake they only met ONCE! And he was from Mayo for goodness sake! I mean – how cool could he have been? The way Sean went on about him you would swear Nadine that it was James Bond he had met! And would you believe, after always telling me that he hated body art of any kind – 'not for those who promote good hygiene' – 'apparently' – he went off and got himself an ugly tattoo on his left forearm. And guess what it was? It said *"My Mama says, to get things done, you better not mess with Major Tom!"* All in aid of his new best friend Thomas of course. And of course from a song by one of Thomas's favourite artists. Such rubbish!"

"Childish!" said Nadine.

"Exactly! replied Yvonne. "And to think all I did for him. Giving him my virginity. Introducing him to you all. Bringing him to my home, to my Ma and Da. Helping him with his studies. Going to Castlebar with him. Getting him All-Ireland tickets. I'm glad they bloody lost now!"

"Yea, up Meath!" laughed Nadine, and the two of them tipped their wine classes together and ordered another two drinks.

"And you mentioned that he neglected you. And that he made excuses not to spend nights with you" said Nadine, "Do you think there was somebody else?"

"I don't know. I just don't know" responded Yvonne, starting to sob again. "I mean...we had been good together. We had been happy together, until that bloody weekend and that bloody crash. It was like he returned from Castlebar a different man. He started missing lectures. And even when he did turn up you could see he was day-dreaming. And then he would be writing down song lyrics on his notes. I sat beside him a couple of days; I saw it with my own eyes. I mean, it was ridiculous what was going on. And he had always complained about money and all of a sudden he seemed to have plenty, and he was spending more and more time in the betting shop."

"Maybe he had a big win?" enquired Nadine.

"I don't think so, but maybe he did. I don't know what to think anymore. I wouldn't say he had another woman on the go though. But maybe I am being silly and stupid. He obviously thought I was stupid!" sobbed Yvonne, as her friend drew closer and put her arm around her.

"You are a bright girl. HE is the stupid one!" said Nadine as she pulled Yvonne in closer to her chest. "Good riddance. You are better off without him. You REALLY are. You deserve only the very best in life. And far from 'the best' he is. His loss!"

"Thanks Nadine" said Yvonne, wiping her eyes with a tissue and drawing back gently into her own seat. "You are my true friend. It's so good to see you. Sometimes I think I am going mad, but now that you are here with me I feel so much better."

"Mad? YOU? If Yvonne Griffin starts going mad then God help the rest of us!" replied Nadine to laughter.

"Speaking of 'other women' and 'going mad' Nadine" said Yvonne, "A strange thing happened one day about two weeks ago."

"Go on" said Nadine, before sipping more wine.

"One day, I decided to finish class early and go to Sean's house. He had not turned up AGAIN so I decided that I'd better check in on him. I KNOW he was there, I just KNOW it. But he did not answer the doorbell or my knocks. Then, I looked up at his bedroom window in case I would see the curtains moving or something. And there was this girl looking down at me..."

"I knew it!" said Nadine.

"No. No, it's not like that" said Yvonne. "Goodness, it was so strange. She was only about six or seven. With long uncombed hair. And she looked SO sad. She was like something you would see in a horror movie. She was SO pale and really had the saddest eyes."

"Jesus!" replied Nadine. "Are you sure it was HIS house? Did you mention it to him?"

"No. It was definitely his house alright, and I dared not mention it to him as he was being very tetchy with me. Goodness knows, we were arguing enough. I did not want to drag that girl into it. Maybe she was the landlord's daughter or something. I did not want him to accuse me of spying on him. But it was so eerie, Nadine. The look she gave me sent shivers down my spine."

As the girls left the hotel bar together for the bus back to Clontarf, Sean was alighting from his bus in Castlebar, where his mother was waiting to greet her firstborn. A month away from him had been a lot for her to endure, and she gave him the warmest of embraces. Back at home, he was also welcomed by his father, sister and grandfather, and the family settled down for a cosy night. The events of four weeks earlier were purposely not mentioned, and the topics of Christmas and Castlebar gossip dominated. Deep down they all wished for a less eventful weekend. As he prepared to rest in his own Castlebar bed, Sean kissed the rosary beads and prayed that Mary Beth had not followed him from Dublin. He had momentarily forgotten that she was a Mayo ghost. But on this occasion, his prayers would be answered.

CHAPTER 20

Saturday 2nd November, 1996

As Teeko's orange Opel Manta slowed down in passing the quaint well-kept village of Bangor Erris, the front seat passenger was deep in thought. Sean was wondering how come so much had changed since he was last with his friends Teeko, Dexter and Jamesie. Even though it was only a month, it might as well have been a year. He was already getting fed up of the name 'Daithí' because they mentioned him so much. Their new friend. It was as if his three friends had signed up to 'The Cult of Daithí'.

That mild morning, the four Castlebar lads were on their way to the Mullet Peninsula on the north-west corner of Mayo. Daithí had invited them to his local golf course there, Carne. He had promised them that they would not regret their effort, that the links course would be their greatest challenge, and that they would never have thought it possible that golf could be played in such a scenic setting.

As the others continued to chatter excitedly about Daithí, Sean found himself feeling a kind of jealousy. And annoyance. A month previously, the same friends had slagged him when he declared his admiration for Thomas Goy. Now, it was clear to him that the three of them were under the spell of this Daithí fellow. It was "Daithí said this, Daithí did that, Daithí thinks this". Who is this guy? Sean vaguely remembered the big Belmullet man serving him drink in his role as a barman in Rockys Bar in Castlebar, but since then it seemed that he had progressed to some type of superhero.

He decided to ask the lads what was so special. They did their best to fill him in, but Sean already had decided that he did not like Daithí, that he would not be enlisting in his fan club. He was told that the new subject of their adulation came from near Blacksod on the southern tip of the Mullet Peninsula. He was a former Irish Junior Boxing Champion who was known as 'Dashing Daithí Donaghy' and he had only missed out on Olympic qualification because of an injury incurred when playing for the Erris United soccer team. Of course, his soccer skills were so

107

good that he had featured on Irish under-age panels. Since moving to work in Rockys Bar there had been attempts by Castlebar Celtic to sign him up, but he had resisted so as to remain loyal to his local club. He was a "class golfer too", as well as a Connaught Darts Champion. He also was a Mayo snooker champion. And had a black belt in Karate. "There seems to be no end to this man's talents" Sean muttered under his breath, before being told that Daithí was also "a great man for the women" – how ever he had time to fit them into his life!

As the first inlets of the Atlantic came into view at Glencastle, Sean remembered Thomas's advice to visit the Erris area of North West Mayo "to sample its savage scenery". He felt as if he was carrying out some last orders for the Ballycroy man. He wondered if Thomas had known this 'Dashing Daithí Donaghy' character. He surely would have mentioned him at some stage if he was as big a star as the lads were making him out to be. Anyway, he could not possibly be as great a "man for the women" as Thomas was.

Daithí and his brother Marc were parked by The Square in Belmullet as previously arranged, and they remained in their golden Fiat Ritmo and led the visitors through the town and onto the peninsula towards Carne Golf Course. Sean's three companions in the Opel Manta were like excited little groupies as they tailed the Fiat Ritmo, as they wondered what the great Daithí had planned for their day. Sean rolled down his passenger window and inhaled the cold sea salt air, and felt his senses become instantly refreshed. He admired the beauty of the water and surrounding green landscape, dotted with proudly maintained houses. In the distance he could see the outline of the mountains of the Nephin range and Achill Island. He began to feel better about the prospect of a day with the wonderful Daithí. But he would not be genuflecting!

Their round of golf proved to be an idyllic experience. Against the backdrop of the Inishkea Islands and Inishglora planted in the Atlantic, the six of them enjoyed the challenges that the sand dunes and hillocks presented. The cold air that breezed in from the sea certainly "blew away any cobwebs", and as they headed for the impressive clubhouse they all felt much more invigorated than they did at the beginning of the round. Playing in a patch touched personally by God himself had done them no harm whatsoever.

Sean had won the round, beating 'the great' Daithí by one shot, so he was particularly upbeat. He had observed "nothing special" about the ex-boxer. He wondered what the fuss was about. Big and broad in stature, Daithí was - in Sean's private opinion – "not an Adonis by any means" – largely thanks to his boxer's flat nose. He did though, ooze confidence. He was quite witty and quick with a quip – but he was not a patch on Thomas!

In the clubhouse, the six treated themselves to some refreshments and sandwiches. The views from the bar were breathtaking as the blue, white and yellow of the sky clashed with the green and gold of the land – as the crashing grey ocean vied for attention. They discussed the tourist potential of the area, and they all agreed that a regular ferry from Blacksod to Achill would be a magnet for tourists. A 'Ring of Mayo' to rival the wondrous 'Ring of Kerry'. Daithí admitted that he was trying to save enough money to set up a bicycle-hire company so as to try and kickstart that element of tourism in the Erris region.

Sean had to admit that Daithí had a charming personality. He always made sure no-one was left out in any conversation. But he was just that bit too 'sure of himself'. Unlike Thomas, he had crossed the border from confidence to cocky. He was having his 21st birthday during the last week of December and he invited them all to come to Belmullet for the celebration. Sean looked on as his mates eagerly accepted.

After a lull in conversation, Teeko asked Daithí if he knew Thomas Goy, saying that he and Sean had attended his funeral. "I just knew him to see. He had left secondary school by the time I started. It was a sad do alright" came the reply. "How come ye were at the funeral?"

"Sean had met him the afternoon he died" responded Teeko before Sean had a chance to answer. "He got a lift from Dublin with him."

"I hope he did not 'drop the hand'!" laughed Daithí.

"What do you mean?" asked Sean.

"Well. I was told he was known by some as 'Thomas Gay'!" replied Daithí, and all bar Sean began laughing as he felt himself go red.

"That explains a lot!" piped up Jamesie as he got a look from Sean that would wither a flower.

"Fuck off!" snarled Sean, growing redder, enraged that anyone would blaspheme his hero like that. "Sure Teeko, you tell them, about all the crying girlfriends at the funeral. That man had more women than there are golf balls in our bags!"

"Ah, it's just what I heard" said Daithí, feeling guilty at how uncomfortable his remark had made Sean.

"And sure women are often a smokescreen for these homosexuals" said Dexter, who was taking pleasure in seeing how a scarlet Sean was squirming. "They say most women feel unthreatened by gays, and that's why you often see so many swarm around them. Sounds like he was a shirt-lifter to me!"

"And weren't you saying you broke it off with Yvonne?" added Jamesie, his comment as unwelcome as a wasp in a wigwam, "Maybe he converted you?"

"It's awful to speak ill of the dead like that!" retorted Sean, trying to control his temper. "I KNOW that he left a trail of bedded women behind him. I have met some of them in Dublin. He was no queer!"

Teeko finally butted in to come to the rescue of his struggling friend, saying that there was "no way Thomas was gay". That rhyming comment in itself received a laugh – from all bar Sean again. Teeko described at how heartbroken the girlfriend Ursula had been at the graveside.

"I wasn't trying to cause any trouble Sean, I was only saying what I heard" said Daithí, trying to get back on track with the man who had just beaten him at golf. "And you're right, we should not be speaking ill of the dead. I apologise. He was obviously a friend of yours and I am very sorry."

"Methinks thou dost protest too much!" quoted the mischievous Dexter.

"Shut up Dexter! I just KNOW that he wasn't a gay" asserted Sean. "And if he had dropped his hand, he would have been killed before he died!" to which there was unanimous laughter. The tension had been broken. But Daithí had one final revelation that riveted Sean:

"A thing I heard about that case actually, just the other night, from a Ballycroy man, is that they have taken in his housemate in Dublin for robbing all of his stuff. He is supposed to have sold off all of his belongings – even his car. The family are very upset. What a thing to do!"

"What do you mean 'taken in'?" asked Sean, gulping.

"Taken in. By the Gardaí! That's what I mean" replied Daithí. "He should rot in jail for doing that. Sure that's worse than grave-robbing!"

"Jesus!" said Dexter, as Teeko looked across at Sean with concern, knowing that this too would upset his friend.

"Maybe yer man was his boyfriend and thinks he is entitled to inherit everything!" laughed Jamesie, dredging up the homosexual angle once more, much to Sean's ire.

"Fuck off Jamesie!" shouted Sean at his fellow Castlebar man, as the clubhouse staff looked on startled. Sean stood up, red-faced, and started wagging his finger in the direction of the sitting Jamesie.

"I have NEVER EVER seen you with a woman so you are some man to talk!" roared Sean. "You are OBSESSED with gays. You talk of NOTHING ELSE! Well, I say 'it takes one to know one'. I DEFY you to get a woman by Christmas. In fact, I BET you can't! You're just A JOKE, Jamesie! You JOKE about a dead man and then you JOKE about him being robbed. You are SICK! Let's see you get a woman now. You have TWO months! Let's see who will be laughing THEN. Let's see who the QUEER is THEN!"

Jamesie was rooted to his chair in shock and embarrassment. Indeed, everyone present was embarrassed. Sean stormed to the orange car and Daithí ushered the rest of them out about a minute later. He meekly waved an apology to the clubhouse staff, feeling guilty that he had invited this outburst upon them.

It was a stone silent car journey back to the Mayo capital for Teeko and Sean in the front and for Jamesie and Dexter in the back. As they sped away from splendid Erris, Teeko opted again to take the Glenisland route as he wanted to avoid the alternative

111

route via Tiernaur – where he had seen the ghost that still gave him nightmares. Not a word was spoken between the four until they went their separate ways in Castlebar, and half-hearted "See yas" were whispered.

Each of the four of them stayed in their homes that night. Sean was seething. Although he was no admirer of Daithí, he did not blame him for the row. The culprit was certainly Jamesie. He had overstepped the mark. Teeko had proved himself to be a true friend, but now he could not give a damn about the other two. Not only had they insulted Sean, but they had insulted the memory of his late friend. Things would never be the same between them.

To console himself, Sean phoned Debbie and spent almost an hour on the phone to her. Her seductive voice promised him a night of pleasure in the coming week, and much more beyond. He was nearing bliss – the consummation of their relationship and the start of something new, promising and exciting. He could not wait to get back to Dublin and lay his eyes upon her dark delectable beauty once more.

Sean was totally besotted. As he drifted off to sleep, it was Debbie that saturated his mind. There was no room to think of the mourning Goy family. No room to think of the heartbroken Ursula, who had learned that Thomas's jacket had yielded only a biro and a torn condom wrapper. Of course she had not realised that jacket was not his. Instead of tormenting her with its suspicion on infidelity, little did she realise her boyfriend's real jacket had contained the keys to a happy future.

Sean's mind had also no room for the plight of the Kerryman Norman. Thomas's loyal housemate and friend. His wrongful arrest had brought shame on his family. Norman was a broken man. He tried to plead his innocence and blame a caller to the house who had passed himself off as a relative. But he had no name, or proof. The caller had arrived and capitalised when Norman was in the depths of despair after hearing that his friend was dead and buried. He suffered from his nerves at the best of times, but now he was on the verge of being admitted to a psychiatric institution. He had lost his mate, his good name, his job, his sanity – and now his freedom.

That night, the angry spirit of Thomas Goy visited Sean in a dream. He warned him to give back all he had stolen and to restore Norman's good name. He warned him to tell Ursula that he had been carrying a diamond engagement ring for her on his final journey, and that he wanted to banish any doubts she had in her mind about his love for her. But by the time morning came, Sean had banished the dream to the back of his mind. Thoughts of the delectable Debbie Willis were now to the forefront, SHE was his ALL.

CHAPTER 21

Saturday 21st December 1996

Sean spent most of the day in the bedroom of his girlfriend Debbie. She was trying to safely navigate the icy pavements of Grafton Street in Dublin, to complete her Christmas shopping, so he had her house to himself. And more importantly, he had her computer to himself. He was getting used of this! Her bedroom was much warmer and cosier than his. He had found his own room back in Drumcondra extra chilly this winter. Even if he had a computer there – and he could well afford one – his digits would be so cold that he would probably not have been able to type properly. In any case, Chucky had become much more bothersome with his unsolicited calls to the Drumcondra house, and it was unlikely he would travel across to the south-side of the city to plague the student.

Not that Sean could justifiably categorise himself as 'a student' anymore. He had only attended an awkward handful of lectures during the previous six weeks, and he had effectively resigned himself to quitting once the summer exams were over. He had the promise of 'a start' with a catering company in early January to cover a maternity leave absence. He still received his weekly payments through the bank from Mayo, and it was still only he that knew of his stockpile of cash. Of course, the amount had been diminished by the £300 he had spent on jewellery and perfume for Debbie. And it was sure to diminish further when he met up with his pals in Castlebar over the Christmas period.

He tried to focus on the typing. It was a slow process. His project was to type out all of the contents of the manuscripts he had found in Thomas's boxes. It was a huge task. He had already given it a month's effort. He had cursed his luck that a convenient computer data disk holding all of the documents had not been found in the cardboard boxes. His fingers ached. His eyes felt strained. So did his neck muscles. He could easily have hired a secretary to do all of the work, but he wanted to become as familiar as he could with Thomas's work, with his innermost thoughts. By transcribing the documents himself he felt that it was almost authenticating his 'rights' over the work. He felt that by osmosis perhaps he would become the talented writer that Thomas was. It was a warped notion, but even Sean himself had to admit that his mind was a warped place these days.

He took a break and looked around the room. He smiled as he spotted some of Debbie's underwear on the carpet. He grinned as he recalled their bedtime activity of the previous night. He was in love.

Debbie was in love too, but not as deeply as Sean was. This was a busy time of year for her and her trade. She had worked long hours. Although she enjoyed his night time company and capability, she was surprised at how many hours he was spending in her place. He always seemed to be there when she left for work, and when she came home. Of course, it was great to have him there to cook for her and he was always generous with little gifts, but she was disappointed that he had apparently quit his studies. She wondered about his ambition. About his long term career prospects. A saving grace was his interest in 'writing' – of course she had been led to believe that he was re-working his own scripts. The fact that Thomas was the creator and author had been conveniently hidden from her.

Throughout the course of her daily work, the striking looking fashion buyer came into contact with many handsome men. Successful men. Normally attired in the best possible threads. Deep down she knew that Sean McRobert was an interim 'arrangement'. Ultimately, the man who would marry her would have to be much more ambitious, stylish and...rich. Nevertheless, she cared for the Mayo man. She had no 'best before end' date in mind. Yet.

Back in her bedroom, Sean was preparing to 'test the water' with the fruits of Thomas's labour. When reading the weekly newspapers from Mayo, which he purchased from Easons when he could, he had noticed a competition for a poem to promote tourism in Mayo. He had been impressed by a poem entitled 'Erris' which Thomas had penned about the barony in North West Mayo that lay adjacent to his home place of Ballycroy. Sean had re-typed the poem, and had doctored it a little, to make it suitable for submission. In a twist he was proud of – he entitled the poem 'Erris-istible'. The submission had to be in by the first week of January, so he was well ahead of time. He rubbed the sheet containing the amended poem against his rosary beads, and smiled as he enveloped his entry.

By this stage, he had a large set of virtual folders created on Debbie's computer. He had them divided and sectored into 'Poems', 'Quotes', 'Songs' and of course the most labour intensive of the lot – Thomas's novel. It had taken fourteen days in a row of intensive typing to get that from sheet to screen. 'The Mayo Ghost Story' was a fascinating tale, set in a retirement home in which the recently-deceased had returned to haunt some of their former 'inmates' – but especially the insufferable staff! It was mostly humorous, but scary in places. Sean knew he had a masterpiece on his hands – and that the story could be adapted and set any where else in the western world. But for the moment, he left it as a Mayo story and title. He had plans to spend further time editing it in the New Year – if his new job permitted!

That evening, before Debbie returned home, Sean went to a nearby phone box at the entrance to Mount Argus. He had two calls to make – one to Teeko and one to his mother. He was still keeping his mobile phone a secret from his mother, and calls to Teeko were cheaper from the coin-box than from his own apparatus.

Teeko filled him in on the local news – who was going out with who, who was breaking up with who, who had got sloshed, what the Christmas week plans were and all of that. Since the day of Thomas's burial, there was 'an elephant in the room' that the two of them did not dare speak about. That was Teeko's sighting of the ghost with the teddy bear. This latest conversation continued that trend. It was a topic none of them felt comfortable discussing. On the topic of females, Teeko confirmed that it was looking like he would have to endure yet another Christmas without a girlfriend!

After completing his call to Teeko, Sean rang his mother who was anxious to find out his plans. As a dutiful housewife, she had a busy schedule for the approaching Christmas week, and needed to know what days her son was due to be around to be fed. Sean filled her in as best as he could. And he was able to tell her that he would be staying in Belmullet for the night of December 28th – the night of the 21st birthday celebrations of 'Dashing' Daithí Donaghy! She replied that Sean's father would also be away that night, he and his mates in Castlebar's Manchester United Fan Club were due to attend the game against Leeds United that day at Old Trafford, so the McRobert girls would have the house to themselves that night!

As Sean tried to bring the conversation to an end, seeing that he was running out of coins to pay for the call, Joan McRobert had two pieces of news that sent Sean back to Debbie's house reeling.

First of all, she said that a young Garda, new to the town of Castlebar, had come to the family door asking if Sean had known the late Thomas Goy.
"What did you tell him?" asked Sean.
"I just said that you had taken a lift from him the evening he died" replied his mother.
"And what else?" asked Sean anxiously?
"Nothing else. Sure I had nothing else to say" she answered.
"And...and did he ask anything else?" asked Sean, now becoming more anxious.
"No. Not really. He just asked if you were still in Dublin and I said that you were" came the reply.
"And did you ask why he was asking for me?" queried Sean.
"No. Not really. I just asked if everything was alright and he said that it was. That it was just normal procedure in the aftermath of an accident. 'Procedure' – yes, that's the word he used" she asserted.

Despite the coldness of the dark December evening in Dublin, Sean felt himself starting to perspire. He did NOT like this development. He struggled with his words and he again tried to terminate the call before his money ran out. But his mother had a second blow:
"And I just heard this evening," she said sadly "That the girlfriend of that lad Thomas who died was found dead last week. An

117

overdose. The poor girl. Ursula, her name was. She could not live without him. What a Christmas for that poor family."

Sean could not find the words to reply. His head was in a tailspin. The phone started beeping as his money ran out. He trudged back to Debbie's, in a daze. Ursula was dead. He felt pangs of guilt. This was dreadful news. It eclipsed the visit by the young Garda to the McRobert homestead. Sean pictured in his head the brown-haired Ursula lying lifeless beside her box of pills. His heart pounded as he thought of her white fingers, robbed of the ring that was meant for her, but was now probably on the finger of a complete stranger. He thought of the thousands of pounds under his bed, which was meant as a deposit for her house. He thought how angry Thomas would be. He expected a horrid dream that night. He deserved a horrid dream.

But in Ballycroy they were living a horrid reality. This was the saddest Christmas anyone could remember. A popular and beautiful couple who should have been enjoying their first Christmas as a betrothed couple were now lying in a soggy cemetery. It was now much too late for the secret guilt of Sean McRobert. His thieving, opportunism and heartlessness had contributed to this appalling outcome. Luckily for him, no one had as yet made the connection. But perhaps this young Garda was onto something? Perhaps he smelled a rat?

The parishioners of the numbed community of Ballycroy compared Thomas and Ursula to 'Romeo and Juliet'. But it was a quote from another Shakespeare play that bounced around the deranged mind of Sean McRobert as it tried to absorb the developments, and the possible consequences. It was a quote that Sean had found amongst the many that Thomas had stored in the cardboard box. It was a quote from 'King Lear':
"No, you unnatural hags! I will have such revenges on you both
That all the world shall - I will do such things - What they are
yet, I know not; but they shall be the terrors of the earth!"

And as Sean tried to sleep on Debbie's pillow that night, Thomas Goy's very own vengeful quote came to the fore of his mind:
"Don't just get even – get ahead!"

CHAPTER 22

Sunday 22nd December 1996

Sean was back in his cold Drumcondra bedroom, packing his belongings for the bus journey to Mayo. He planned to travel the next day. He carefully placed the gift he had for Debbie into his rucksack. They would have a romantic night together before he headed west, and she headed east to the United Kingdom.

As he focused on his preparations, and what to do with his stash of cash, he had momentarily pushed aside his guilt over Ursula's death. And his annoyance that the young Mayo Garda had been making enquiries about him. But a knock to the door downstairs would increase his annoyance.

The visitor was Chucky, dressed as usual in a tattered jacket and paint-splattered tracksuit pants, stinking again from alcohol and looking rougher than ever. Sean thought he could see icicles on parts of his scruffy hair. His nose looked so flat that Sean wondered how the man could inhale. The Dubliner was rubbing his hands as if to warm himself up, and he paced the sitting room. All of Sean's housemates had already left for their homes for the Christmas break.

"I am in a hurry, Chucky, what is it you need me for?" asked Sean, wishing he had ignored the knock to the door.
"Now don't yous be hasty, Seanie!" laughed Chucky, still pacing menacingly. "I have some news that might slow you down, Boyo! And I've noticed yous haven't been around these parts too much lately – avoiding me, are yous?"
"I've been around alright!" replied Sean. "Now, out with it, what news have you for me?"
"Not so fast, hold your horses there, hold your horses Boyo!" replied Chucky. "Can yous boil me a cup of tea first?"

Sean switched on the kettle and searched for a clean cup. Or even the cleanest cup. It was a student house after all! He was hoping that he would have 'escaped' back to Mayo before Chucky visited again. No doubt the old codger was looking for more money.

Sean had even feared that Chucky would burgle the place and find his stash.

"Garda Gilligan has been asking about yous?" said Chucky. Sean was visibly taken aback. First, the young Garda enquiring in Mayo, and now this?!
"Who the hell is Garda Gilligan and how does he know me?" shouted Sean.
"Ha – I knew that might upset yous!" laughed the ugly IRA sympathiser. "Not so calm now, are you Boyo? Well, to answer your question, Garda Gilligan is the main peeler around these parts. He's a sergeant actually. But he's not the worst – sure he is a culchie too like yous!"
"But why is he interested in ME?" asked Sean as the kettle began to boil. "Is it the car? Is it the fecking car? You SAID it would not be traced!"
"Hold your horses, hold your horses Boyo!" yelled Chucky. "It can't be the car. That was a professional job I assure yous! It must be something else – like the dodgy fifty pound notes yous have been passing in the bookies! And by the way, yous would be well advised to choose another bookies, Boyo. Vince and the girls are not happy with yous! Nor are the rest of us! Yous has drawn too much heat on the place with your forgeries!"

Sean was speechless. He tried not to burn himself as he prepared the tea. His hands were shaking. He was beginning to perspire again. He could not believe what he was hearing. As he sipped his tea, the grateful Chucky repeated what he had said, just to see the Mayo man squirm. He was enjoying this! And he was determined to profit from it.

"Now. I'm a decent man. And Garda Gilligan is a decent man. He doesn't want to be bothering us as much as we don't want to be bothering him. He's a sound skin" said Chucky, building up his story.
"What have you told him about me?" asked Sean, horrified.
"I've told him nothing. Nothing YET!" smiled Chucky showing his stained yellow teeth, his ugly eyes peering at the crumbling 20 year old.

"But me and Garda Gilligan go back a long way and have been through a lot together. Just two words from me and something nice in his uniform pocket and he will ask no more questions, know what I mean? He will not ask about yous again. But it will cost you three hundred, Boyo!"

"Three hundred quid?!" shouted the student.

Sean felt sick. He was being blackmailed. And there was little he could do about it. He cursed his own folly at becoming 'involved' with the gruesome gnome that stood in his kitchen. But Chucky had his prey where he wanted him:

"Three hundred for me – AND three hundred for Garda Gilligan and there will be no more questions!" smiled Chucky.

"WHAT?!" roared Sean. "Six hundred fucking quid. Fuck off for yourself! Just fuck off! Let Garda Gilligan ask what he wants but he is getting no Christmas money from me. Sure...if he thinks my money is forged, why would he want that?"

Chucky knew that Sean was bluffing. He watched the beads of sweat roll down his face – even in an arctic kitchen. He watched like a hawk as the bewildered lad pondered his next move. He had a migraine. His head was abuzz with questions. "Two Gardaí in two days. Were they onto him at last?" "Had the Volvo turned up somewhere?" "Had Norman recognised him somewhere around the city?" "Could he trust Chucky – maybe he was a police informer?" "Even if the £600 was handed over, would Chucky not come back for more?" "Had all of Thomas's money been forgeries – surely it could not have been?"

"I better leave so" snarled Chucky. "Maybe I will bump into Garda Gilligan on my way back. I think his Christmas Party was last night!"

"Wait!" said Sean, weighing up his not-so-nice options. "Did he have my full name? Sure you don't even know my full name?"

"McRobert, isn't it?" smiled Chucky. "And I'm not even a detective!" The name inked on Sean's rucksack and on the science workbook left on the window sill were giveaways, but Sean was spooked.

"Do you PROMISE that he will stay away if I give you some money?" he cried.

"Six hundred quid and yous will never hear another word. I swear on my mother's grave!" replied Chucky, trying to look serious, thawing snot dripping down from his nostril towards his upper lip.

Sean ran upstairs and came down within thirty seconds. As soon as he had got rid of Chucky, he would have to remove the rest of the cash from the house because surely Chucky would organise a break-in over the Christmas when the street would be deserted. But his main aim was to get rid of Chucky for now, and by extension the querying of this Garda Gilligan.

"Here. There's a thousand dollars!" he panted, handing over the very envelope that Thomas had used. "Share it between yourself and Garda Gilligan. It probably works out at more than three hundred each but take it to fuck. And off with you! Off to fuck with you!"
"Merry Christmas Mr Lawrence!" laughed Chucky as he was ushered out onto the street. "Yous will not regret this, my culchie friend, yous will not regret this! Happy Christmas Seanie Boy!" and off down the cobblestones he danced.

An angry Sean wiped the sweat from his brow. He felt sick. He was disgusted. He would have to leave this house. For good. He never wanted to lay his eyes on the obnoxious Chucky again. A tear rolled down his cheek as he watched the Dubliner disappear from view. "Gouger" he shouted after him. "You're nothing but a fucking gouger!"

The young man from Castlebar had been conned. But he did not realise the extent of the con. That night, as Sean made his way across the city to Debbie, Chucky sat in his local buying rounds of drink for his many friends, and regaling his story as laughter filled the bar. There had been NO forged fifty pound notes in the bookies. There had been NO enquiries from the Gardaí in Dublin. There had been NO demand for a bribe. Because there was NO Garda Gilligan! But Chucky – for a couple of festive nights at least – would have NO shortage of cash!

CHAPTER 23

Monday 23rd December 1996

Debbie lay across Sean's bare chest. Her quilt was wrapped around them both. The necklace he had bought her sparkled beneath the lit bedside lamp. It was only 6am but they had a busy day ahead, buses and planes to catch. Family presents to finalise.

Debbie was irked as she had not slept as much as she had hoped to or as much as she needed to. Sean had been very restless, tossing and turning throughout the night. She was tired. And she wanted the bedroom to herself as quickly as she could, as she had too much to organise. She made her feelings known to her boyfriend. For whatever reason, maybe because of the succulent gifts she had bought him, he decided it was a good time to tell her about the visitations he had been receiving from the other-worldly waif he now called 'Mary Beth'.

Debbie was astounded. She thought he was joking at first. But then, she could see the genuine fear in his eyes as he described the visitations in detail. The aggression of the ghost. The way it would 'attack' without warning. The vile voice from beyond the grave. The feeling of utter sadness. The way prayer fended it off. She now knew he had a genuine reason for some of his sleeplessness.

"It's when I am still that the problems arise!" he said. "Getting to turn around and twist in the sheets is great. You need to get worried if I'm motionless. Because she paralyses you once she tries to take over".

"Take over? I cannot understand that part. In fact, I cannot understand ANY part of this!" said Debbie, fascinated. "Why does she want to 'take over' YOU?"

"It's like she wants to enter my body, discard my spirit, and take over my spirit and body" continued Sean. "And I have to fight her off because once she takes total control, THEN I will be a gonner! The best way I can describe it, Debbie, is that I feel like a glass of water. Just sitting there on a table. Then, someone comes along and pours orange juice into me and tries to turn me orange. And if I don't fight back, if I let myself become completely orange so to speak, someone will shortly come along and drink me and I will end up 'God knows where'. Do you understand?"

"Not really!" replied Debbie. "And can you blame me? This is WEIRD! I am half African so I guess I should know about voodoo dolls and the likes, but this is just WEIRD!"

Debbie continued her questions and Sean tried to answer as best as he could. He was slightly disappointed that she wasn't being more loving or sympathetic. But it was a BIG thing to tell her. No doubt she had fears that she too might be 'attacked'. She got some comfort from his 'lie' that Mary Beth had not visited him when he was in her house!

"And you say it's a girl, or the spirit of a girl, but you say you cannot see her face. How can that be?" asked a perplexed Debbie.

"It IS difficult to explain, I know" replied Sean. "The best way I can describe that part, is like…like when you hear a song on the radio and you don't know who is singing it. You somehow get a picture in your mind's eye of what the singer may look like, don't you?"

"I suppose" whispered Debbie.

"So, if it's a male singer, the voice may hint whether he is black or white, and then you create an image…prompted by the song … that he may be fat or thin, tall or short, have hair or be bald. Often, you might imagine a completely different person until you get to see the album cover or video, and you might be shocked. Right?"

"I guess" said Debbie.

"Well, from her voice and feelings an image is projected onto my mind that she is a poor, starving, sad little girl. I cannot explain it anymore. I can almost picture her sad eyes and purple mouth, and her straggly hair. It's purely down to sensing it. Put it this way, she is not Barry White, Mister T or The Refrigerator! She is a small, weak little thing. I just sense it."

Debbie had plenty of time to try and digest Sean's revelations as she sat on the airplane to Heathrow. The absurd story had increased her doubts about her relationship with him. She would think more about it over Christmas in Hounslow and make a decision in January. For now, she just wanted to enjoy a reunion with her family and friends. Little did she know that her Dublin bedroom had just become home to a hidden shoebox containing over seven thousand pounds!

On the packed bus to Mayo, Sean was concentrating on using the 'text message' facility on his mobile phone. Some of his friends now had invested in mobiles also, so this was a novel and convenient way of communication. 'Texting' had helped soothe his argument with Dexter and put their friendship back on track. He was looking forward to meeting up with the lads and having their traditional pub crawl on Christmas Eve. For a change this year, he would not be short of money and would not have to try and squeeze some from his father. He was still anxious though, to see his father again, plus of course his loving mother and his sister Gracie. And his grandfather.

As he centred his yuletide thoughts on himself and his family, there was no place in his thoughts for the mourning families of Ballycroy. Those left behind by Thomas and Ursula were united in grief. What should have been the happiest time of year was becoming an increasing black burden of brónach – the gaelic word for sadness.

Anthony Goy visited the grave of his beloved brother. He sobbed on the Ballycroy hillside cemetery as he remembered the joyous days spent playing and laughing with Thomas. In between his tears, he tried to tell him that he would look after their parents. That he would do his only sibling proud. That he would someday soon bring a sister-in-law to the grave to introduce them. And that in years to come he would make sure that nephews and nieces would pay pilgrimage to the headstone of the uncle they never got to meet.

In Dundrum's Mental Hospital, Norman O'Toole cried too. His elderly parents and his sisters had just left for the long trip back to Kerry after visiting their incarcerated son and brother. They cried too for the plight of their Norman. He cried because he could not believe that he was STILL inside, trying to retain his sanity in the midst of REAL lunatics. "Christmas in Hell". He regretted physically hitting out at the Gardaí who accused him of stealing the belongings of his dead house-mate. He regretted threatening the landlord who had insinuated the same thing. He regretted threatening Anthony Goy when he bluntly accused him of being a 'grave-robbing thief'. Norman KNEW that he was being blamed in the wrong. He KNEW that he could never do such an awful thing. He KNEW that somehow, someway, he had to escape and clear his name. He KNEW that he would have to track down the REAL thief. He KNEW that he would have to convince his family that he did not deserve to be back in psychiatric care again.

In Clontarf, Yvonne shed a tear as she looked at photographs of her and Sean together just months earlier, in happier times. She was dreading Christmas without him, even though she knew it was for the best. She had sent a card to his home in Mayo, but it was looking as if he had not bothered to reciprocate. She was right. As Nadine had said "Sean is just a self-centred bollix." The approaching year of 1997 promised to be kinder to this daughter of Dublin with a heart of gold. But Yvonne was still heartbroken: "If only that damned car had not stopped to pick Sean up..."

As the bus neared his well-lit Christmassy home town, Sean had promised himself that this would be an enjoyable yuletide. The events of the past few months – good and bad – would be temporarily left aside. But he remembered Thomas as he hummed one of his favourite tunes by one of his favourite artists: *"I've never done good things, I've never done bad things,*
I never did anything out of the blue, Want an axe to break the
ice, Want to come down right now.."

To Sean, Bowie's lyrics seemed more apt than any festive ditty...

CHAPTER 24

Saturday 28th December 1996

"What time will you be home tomorrow, will you be back for dinner time?" asked Joan McRobert as her son rushed out the door towards Teeko's revving car.

"As Gazza once said 'I don't make predictions – and I never will!'" laughed Sean. "Will see you when I see you! Byeeee!"

"Who the hell is 'Gazza'?" asked his mother as the door slammed.

The four friends were on their way to Belmullet for the 21st birthday celebrations of 'Dashing' Daithí Donaghy. And they were staying there overnight. The dull wintry shades of winter contrasted sharply with the blur of glowing orange that came from Teeko's sports car as it sped through the countryside. Again, he refused a request from Sean to take the coastal route. He wanted to avoid the spot where he had seen the ghost. He would instead drive to Belmullet via the imposing tower of Bellacorick's peat power station. It dominated the surrounding brown flat landscape.

Sean, Teeko, Jamesie and Dexter were in fine giddy form. They were looking forward to their night in a new town, the nightlife of which they had never previously sampled. Sean recalled the advice he received from Thomas to go and explore that part of the world. He was 'following orders' – this would be his second trip to the barony of Erris in three months! He wasn't as close to Daithí as the other three were, but he was looking forward to a change of scenery nonetheless. They had downed pints in almost every pub in Castlebar during their socialising on the nights of December 24th, 26th and 27th!

As with their previous trip, every story that his three Castlebar-based companions told seemed to feature Daithí in some way. Sean felt slightly jealous but he decided not to make any comment that might reveal that emotion. Instead, he decided to target their chauffeur to maintain the banter:

"All set for some 'inloxicating tiquour' tonight then Teeko?!"

"Feck off!" laughed his target, adding "Sure don't I deserve a right drink at last? I've been taxi-ing ye shower all week. Now I hope ye return the favour by filling my petrol tank up!"

"Where is it we're staying tonight?" asked Jamesie.

"Daithí said that his brother-in-law, the Italian fella, I forget his name again, is putting us up in his brand new house just beyond the town of Belmullet" replied Dexter.

"That must be Umberto, he often mentions him" said Teeko. "At least it's free. Should be a nice gaffe if it's only newly-built."

"Umberto!" said Sean. "Bet there aren't many with that name around Belmullet! How on earth does an Italian end up out here like that?!"

His companions laughed and as they passed through the village of Bangor Erris they continued to tease the unfortunate Teeko about his past mispronunciation howlers:

"Remember when you asked Gerry White if he and his new bride had 'constipated the marriage'?!" said Dexter to roars of laughter.

"And....and what about...what about the time" said Jamesie trying to compose himself, "What about the time you called his brother Shane White 'Wayne Shite'?!" and more hilarity ensued at the scarlet Teeko's expense.

"You have to admit that WAS priceless!" said Sean, touching Teeko's left shoulder. "The poor man had to emigrate – he could never live that name down!"

"And did you hear that he married an Australian girl called Aggie over in Sydney?" asked Dexter.

"Didn't know that" replied Teeko.

"Yea. It's true alright" said Dexter as he tried to perfect the timing of his punchline. "Shane and Aggie – or as they are known on Bondi Beach : Shaggie!"

The merriment continued as darkness descended and the four completed their fifty mile journey. With the help of directions from a friendly local they easily located Umberto's house and the effusive host gave them a warm welcome before showing them to their rooms. The smell of fresh paint and wood resin filled their senses as they received a quick tour of the house, but soon the fumes of their deodorant and aftershave were totally dominant. It wasn't long before they were enjoying their first pint in

Leneghan's Bar. They had decided to sample a few of the local hostelries before joining Daithí at his party.

In the bar of The Western Strands Hotel on Belmullet's main thoroughfare they watched some of the highlights of the soccer games that had taken place that day in England:
"That's the game my father was at today" said Sean as the big screen in the bar showed the action from Old Trafford.
"At least United won, Cantona, a penalty" said Jamesie.
"So THAT is why you were driving around in your father's car today, looking 'As Happy as Larry'!" said Teeko. "When the cat's away the mouse will play!" and the others laughed.
"By the way" added Teeko, "You were lucky the guards weren't around, they were probably too hungover to be on duty!"
"What do you mean?" asked Sean, supping from his pint.
"The guards. The Gardaí. You are lucky they weren't pulling cars today or they would have stopped you" replied Teeko as the others looked on.
"Sure what would I have to worry about?" asked Sean. "Sure, I have my licence, and the car is taxed and insured...."
"No – not that!" laughed Teeko. "The girleen. That's why!"
"The girleen? What do you mean?" asked Sean, wondering if the alcohol was beginning to already adversely affect Teeko.
"The girl. The girl who was in the car with you. She was sitting in the front! She's much too young to be sitting in the front. Who was she anyway – your cousin?" came the reply.
"What the hell are you on about?" responded Sean, getting annoyed as Teeko was distracting him from the football action. "I was on my own. It must have been some other car you saw!"
"No. DEFINITELY. You passed up the town at about 3 O'clock, yea? I was standing outside McCarthys but I knew you didn't see me. And there was a girl – aged about five or six – in the passenger seat beside you. For sure!" asserted Teeko.
"Don't say you don't remember a girl being in the car with you!" interjected Jamesie, but there was no response from Sean as he fixed a glare on his pint. He felt a chill. He felt the hairs on the back of his neck stand. He looked up at Teeko, whose attention was now drawn to an incident in the football match.

After a few minutes, when he got Teeko's attention back, he beckoned to him to follow him out into the hotel's hallway. Their companions were focused fully on the match, and had not taken any notice of their departures.

"Listen. Teeko! growled Sean in a hushed voice. "Don't fecking mess with my head, OK! Now. Tell me the truth. You better not be messing. Did you see a girl in my car?!"

I did! I swear I did!" responded the startled fellow, wondering why Sean looked upset. He had not seen him this upset since…

"Oh no – oh no! Oh hell no!" said Teeko as he copped on to what was agitating his friend. "Not ANOTHER fucking ghost! No! No! No! What the hell is this, WHY ME? I am going to get sick – where is the fucking jacks…?" and off he ran. The sweat poured from Sean as he leaned against the wall, ignoring the inquiries about his welfare from the passing concerned hotel staff.

He was in shock. Teeko had spotted 'Mary Beth'. She had been in the car with him! He felt faint. He stumbled to the nearby staircase and sat on the third step, his wet head in his hands.

After several minutes, a pale Teeko emerged from the bathroom. He spotted his friend on the stairs and sat beside him.

"ANOTHER ghost of yours!" he said quietly. "What the hell are you doing to me? I still can't sleep after the last one. How come YOU cannot see them but I DO?!"

"I don't know!" whispered Sean. "I just don't know. She has been haunting me. I don't really see her but I can sense her. She never reveals herself to me like she did to you."

"Well, I should think not!" replied Teeko with a nervous laugh. "I doubt you would be driving around all day smiling if you could see her beside you! I just got a second or two of a glance. But NOW she will be with me forever. Just like HIM. The man with the teddy bear. I swear Sean I see him everyday. He seems to pop up everywhere – just for a second. And then disappear. Just like that. He is always in my dreams as well. Oh no, I just can't fucking believe this is happening again. I need a drink. And food. I have just puked my guts up in there!"

"Does the spirit, does he try and take you over?" asked Sean, wondering if Teeko might have been receiving the same visitations he had.

"No. He just appears. Looking sad. But not as sad looking as that girl today. My God, she looked so sad. I assumed it was one of your little cousins – frozen with fear because of your awful driving skills!" laughed Teeko but Sean was not in the form to join.

"Long hair, lonesome eyes, gaunt expression – yea?" asked Sean.

"That was her alright" answered Teeko.

"I've christened her 'Mary Beth'. She haunts me. It's awful. I will tell you again some other night – but you are right, we need to get food. My stomach has just drained. My veins have just drained!" said Sean, and off they went to the nearest takeaway, leaving their bewildered friends behind.

Over their burgers and chips at 'Snoopys' they compared ghost experiences. They rejoined Dexter and Jamesie after forty minutes, and the four of them enjoyed a few drinks with the locals in McDonnells Bar. By 10.30pm they were at Daithí's party in The Anchor Hotel. He was delighted to see them and gave each one a tight bear hug. The four lads were impressed – great location, great food, great music and above all – great women! Daithí was a popular figure and the finest females from the far-flung factories and farms of North Mayo were present, in their glamorous best. The night promised much!

The tall Daithí was in great demand, and was clearly enjoying all of the attention.   Sean was impressed as midnight neared when the ex-boxing champion took time out to sit beside him for a few minutes, despite the demands that were on him from all of his guests:

"Thanks for coming. I hope you are enjoying the night."

"I am indeed, just taking a breather from the dance floor!" replied Sean. "More importantly, I hope YOU are enjoying the party!"

"I am indeed. Great turnout. Must be two hundred here!" said Daithí proudly, leaning his chair back against the wall and surveying the crowd. "Did you hear that I'm off to join the Gardaí in a few weeks?"

"No?! Really?!" exclaimed Sean. "That's GREAT news. Well done!"

"Thanks. And I will be onto you for digs if they station me in Dublin!" replied Daithí. "I hope I get ANYWHERE but Dublin. Accommodation is far too expensive up there."

"It is, but it's a great city" replied Sean.

"For cowboys like you perhaps, but not for sheriffs like me!" joked Daithí nudging him and laughing. "Listen, wasn't it awful about Thomas Goy's girlfriend?"

"Sad news alright" replied Sean.

"And I'm sorry about that 'gay' lark from before, I never meant to cause any upset" said Daithí apologetically.

"No worries. You were only quoting what you had heard" replied Sean. "By the way, did you hear if they caught who robbed his belongings?"

"Well, I heard his housemate is still 'inside' for it, so it must be him" answered Daithí, swigging from his bottle.

"Look at yer man there!" continued Daithí, changing the subject, "Have you ever laid your eyes on such an idiot in your life?!"

"The stumpy sweaty old fella with the glitzy shirt, the beer-belly and the ponytail?! Yea, I wasn't going to say anything in case he was a relation of yours!" laughed Sean.

"A RELATION?! No fecking way!" exclaimed Daithí. "The shagger wasn't even invited!"

"Really? What's he doing here so? Why don't you get the bouncers to throw him out?" enquired Sean as the music continued to blare in the background.

"Not worth it!" came the reply. "He turns up at EVERY thing. He is a journalist, a self-styled 'gossip columnist' in the local rag. Don't say anything to him or he might quote you! He's just a prize idiot. He keeps boasting about his high readership figures but the truth is that so many people get a kick out of seeing him make a complete ass of himself every week!"

Sean laughed as he studied the subject of Daithí's outburst.

"He looks like he should be at home with his pipe and slippers by the Christmas tree and not trying to make himself out to be a young one" he added. "The shirt and the ponytail are hideous. You would think someone would tell him to cop himself on, wouldn't you?"

"And as for my bouncers" continued Daithí after swigging more alcohol, "Have you realised that there are FOUR of them?!"

"Four?" replied Sean. "I thought there were just two!"

"Common mistake!" laughed Daithí. "See – one there, one over there, another one over there and then a fourth one outside! The Hanrahans. Two sets of cousins. More idiots – see their walkie talkies and headphones – you'd swear it was Chelsea Clinton's 21st they were patrolling and not mine!"

"They all look identical!" giggled Sean.

"Exactly. All thick-necked brothers and cousins. Seamus and Eamonn Hanrahan, and Raymond and Damien Hanrahan. Or as they are known by the locals around here 'Shaymo, Eaymo, Raymo and Daymo'!" laughed Daithí, rising from his seat as he was led to the floor by a buxom blonde, the sound of The Spice Girls' latest 'Two Become One' signalling that 'the slow set' had started.

Sean was still laughing about the bouncers when the drunken Teeko stumbled to the chair that Daithí had just left:

"I need to go to bed, Sean, I am pissed!"

"OK, we will slip away!" replied Sean as he finished his pint. And as the two of them left the party they saw that Dexter and Jamesie were having a 'better than usual' night as each of them wrapped their arms around girls from Erris on the dance floor – Jamesie was even kissing his new friend! He was proving to Sean that he was 100% heterosexual alpha male – and not just all talk! There would be slagging about this in the morning...

CHAPTER 25

Sunday 29th December 1996

It was nearly 1am by the time Sean started to sleep. He was sharing a room with Teeko, who was already snoring. He thought that he would probably be awoken by their two friends when they returned later on, but luckily for them they both had cause to spend the night elsewhere.

About an hour later, Sean felt himself trapped in a horrendous dream. He tried to wake, but felt himself unable to. His head was filled with horrifying fiendish screams – a mixture of angry male, screeching female and howling beast. It was like they were arguing in an incomprehensible language. As if they were competing to take over him. Again, Sean felt himself entirely paralysed. He was lying on his side. This was not 'Mary Beth' – but something much more aggressive and dangerous. He could sense that whatever was attacking his soul had only pain in mind. He managed to open one eye, his right eye, to look at the wall in front of him, which was partly lit by light that came from a gap in the curtains from a streetlight. His left eye was buried in the pillow. His tongue became numb again as he tried to remember the words to some prayers, but as the screams continued he was unable to muster a prayer – even in his mind. Had he finally been taken over?

Sean knew that this was an altogether different experience. Whereas with 'Mary Beth' the overwhelming feelings were of fear and supreme sadness, the feeling now one was of pure badness. Overpowering and overwhelming evil. Then, he felt his legs being pulled. He felt as if he was being dragged from the bed by powerful forces. He tried to kick away his supernatural aggressors but he was powerless to move. He felt himself levitate above the bed as he was being pulled towards an air vent in the corner of the room, through which some of the streetlight rays were also coming.

This time, Sean felt that he was in a spiritual struggle that he would lose, that even the power of prayer could not save him. This was different. Frightening in the extreme. He looked down

134

from near the ceiling and could see his body on the bed below, still lying sideways. He could see his clothes and shoes on the floor. He tried to cry out but he wasn't able to. He slowly passed over the snoring Teeko below. He was mortified. Was this the end? Was he being taken to Satan? In his ears he could still hear the yells from hell. Roars from the depths of despair. He wondered what would happen once his feet hit the wall. Would his body be squeezed through the air vent? Would he just bypass the wall? What was outside the wall – in the light? Where would he be taken to?

Just as his feet approached the wall a large moan came from the mouth of Teeko below, and in a millisecond Sean was back in his bed. Back in his own body. It was as if the noise from Teeko disturbed the evil spirits and they just dropped him. Sean sat up in his bed, panting. He knew that it had not just been a nightmare. He thanked God for Teeko's moan, and looked over at the outline of his sleeping friend. He looked up at the air vent and the thin yellow lines of light that crossed it. He wondered if the spirits were outside waiting for him. He was exhausted from his 'struggle' against them. He could still sense their menace, their sinister intent. He tried to sleep again but he was shaking. All of a sudden, a louder groan came from Teeko's bed. It sounded mournful.
"Are you OK Teeko?" whispered Sean sitting up. He strained his ear and once he heard a deep breath come from Teeko again his mind was put at ease and he instantly fell asleep. The eight pints from the evening helped!

It was 5am when Sean clumsily navigated his way to the toilet to get rid of some of that gallon. And not long after 8am when nature called again. Much more alert this second time, he checked the room in Umberto's house that Dexter and Jamesie were due to sleep in and smiled to himself as he found both beds undisturbed. Back in his and Teeko's room, he decided that at least another hour's sleep was in order. He grimaced as he recalled the violent visitation of a few hours earlier. But minutes later he was back in a deep slumber again.

His dreams were disturbed when Jamesie entered the room at 9.30am. He shook Sean, waking him, anxious to boast about his conquest:

"And you defied Dexter and me to get women!" he laughed, making his way to shake Teeko from his slumber. "I got off with a fine bit of stuff – did you see her, did you see her Sean?"

"Fair play to you!" laughed Sean, sitting up and rubbing his eyes. "What is her name and how much did you pay her?!" But Jamesie didn't respond as expected.

"Will you wake up, Teeko" he uttered as Sean started asking if he knew of Dexter's whereabouts.

"Shut up Sean!" responded Jamesie.

"What the fuck is wrong with YOU?!" asked Sean, rising from the bed. "I thought you'd be happy now at last that you got yourself a woman!"

"WAKE UP! WAKE UP TEEKO!" shouted Jamesie as it struck Sean that something terrible was wrong. He walked over to the single bed beneath the air vent and window where Jamesie was struggling to wake their friend. The curly-haired rotund Castlebar man looked up at Sean with dread in his eyes:

"He's not breathing, Sean, he's not fucking breathing!"

"Check his pulse!" urged Sean as his mouth began to dry up.

"I think he's dead! I think Teeko's dead!" cried Jamesie.

Sean was dumbstruck. He recalled the groans from the night and looked down at the white face of Teeko. His eyes were closed. He looked liked a waxwork model. This could NOT be happening!

"I SAID – ring a fucking AMBULANCE!" shouted Jamesie as Sean's trembling fingers searched his jeans for his mobile phone. He dialled 999. When the operator asked where he needed an ambulance for he did not know the number of the house, or the address, or the surname of the owner. He ran down the corridor in his underpants and burst open every door until he found Umberto and Daithí's sister, who were not happy to have their hangovers activated so quickly:

"Where are we? We need an ambulance!" croaked Sean. "What's your name, Umberto?"

"What the hell do you mean 'what's my name'!" snarled the Italian. "You just said my fucking name!"

"I mean – what's your surname? Sorry, your surname, your surname for the ambulance?!" roared Sean in a panic.

"Di Martino, Di Martino!" yelled Umberto as he rose naked from his bed. "And what the hell is going on?!"

Within 10 minutes a doctor had arrived and was trying to revive Teeko. It was only then that a stunned Sean noticed the trickle of blood from Teeko's left ear onto the pillow below. A stench of urine came from the poor lad as the doctor worked furiously on him. They could hear the ambulance sirens approach in the distance, awakening virtually the whole town.

Umberto and his wife tried to console Sean and Jamesie. No one could believe that the joviality of the party was now replaced by this utter unimaginable unfolding horror.

"Please, please let him live!" cried Sean. "My God, how are we going to tell his mother and father? HOW Jamesie?! I heard him groan, a couple of times, I should have checked him. I hope he didn't vomit in his sleep. Oh no, oh no..."

As unreal as this was, Sean was unable to disclose about his ghostly experience. He wondered if it had been the spirits who tried to take him who had now come back and taken Teeko. After all, it was the first moan from Teeko that fended them off from him.

Ambulance personnel rushed into the room and soon paramedics offered their assistance to the dishevelled looking doctor, who just shook his head.

"A haemorrhage or an aneurysm I'd say. May he rest in peace." The words rocked Sean. He felt like he had just been hit by a wrecking ball.

"Oh no!" he cried mournfully as he rushed over to Teeko's body. Umberto grabbed him and before long the wailing Sean was under sedation. He was not able to cope with the shock of his longest friend just dying beside him. It was just too much.

It fell to Dexter to telephone the Murphy family in Castlebar to break the awful news. Dexter also accompanied Teeko on his sad return journey back to his native town in the hearse. Umberto arranged for a sober friend to drive Sean and Jamesie back to their homes. A crying Daithí hugged them both as the dumbstruck pals entered the jeep. Neighbours and friends gathered around the upset Umberto and Deirdre. What an awful thing to happen in their newly-built home. The Gardaí examined the room and prepared for a trip to the morgue in Castlebar, where they also intended to interview Teeko's three friends.

For the rest of his days, the events immediately after Teeko's death were a blur to Sean. Medication and heartbreak combined to reduce him to a sobbing shell. He could barely remember being interviewed by the Gardaí, who were satisfied that there was no foul play. The County Coroner was to rule the cause of death as being a cerebral aneurysm. A groan such as Sean heard – and which too haunted him – was common enough in such situations.

As bad as he reacted to the death of Thomas Goy, he reacted much worse to the death of Sean 'Teeko' Murphy. His family and friends gathered around him but all his thoughts were for his oldest friend, who had been taken so suddenly away. Calls of comfort from Debbie in England could do nothing to ease his pain. As the devastated Castlebar public looked on at Sean's visible grief, little did they know of the thoughts that tormented him – that perhaps poltergeists had come and taken his best friend instead of him.

Tuesday 31st December 1996

The popular Murphy family were distraught as their loved son and brother was laid to rest in Castlebar. His beloved orange Opel Manta – driven by a devastated Daithí – led the hearse and coffin into the graveyard. Hundreds gathered to say goodbye to the skinny baldy smiley figure who had bejewelled all of their lives. It was the cruellest way for any family to end a year – and to face into a whole new one.

Sean stood by the graveside, supported by Dexter and Jamesie. In fact they were all leaning on each other – physically as well as emotionally. He tried to come to terms with Teeko's poignant passing. He felt guilty – even though he was receiving almost as much sympathy from the supportive community as the Murphys were. Tears fell from his eyes onto the icy clay as he recalled their final conversation about ghosts. He wondered why the spectres of the man with the teddy bear and the waif Mary Beth had appeared to Teeko but not to him. Perhaps they only reveal themselves to those about to join them in death? What a few months this had been. Sean was beginning to now regret ever taking that lift that afternoon. And he was beginning to also regret all he had stolen from the dead man. It could not have been just a coincidence that Teeko had just died weeks after Thomas's girlfriend had. Maybe this was Thomas's way of 'getting even'? "My God" thought Sean, "If this is his way of getting even, what on earth is he going to do to me in order to get ahead?"

CHAPTER 26

Friday 28th February 1997

For the third time in four months Sean McRobert found himself back in Belmullet by the sea. This time, it was a bittersweet trip. The late Thomas – who came from Ballycroy some 25 miles away - and of course the late Teeko, were both on his mind that evening. But he was in the company of five fine-looking women, so they helped distract him as he tried to calm his nerves. For Sean was attending a function that was being held in his honour – as winner of the newspaper competition for the best poem to promote Mayo! 'Erris-istible' had come up trumps!

A crowd of over 200 people gathered on the basketball court of Belmullet's Community Centre to see 'The Poet' accept his award of a sculpted trophy and £1,000! Sean, dressed immaculately in a navy suit, white shirt and gold tie – all purchased with Thomas's money – sat at a table facing the audience. He was flanked by the newspaper editor and the sculptor, and a number of local dignitaries were also present. He had a wry smile to himself when he spied the outrageously dressed 'gossip columnist' with the sweaty forehead, protruding paunch and pathetic ponytail enter the arena. He looked as ridiculous as ever, holding his notepad and doing a headcount of the attendees. Sean gulped nervously and began to perspire himself when he saw the microphone being prepared. He would have to recite 'his' poem and say a few words to those who had braved the cold evening to attend. When it became known amongst the Belmullet community that the winning poet had shared a bedroom with the tragic Teeko the night he passed away, they ensured he was even more warmly welcomed.

His mother Joan and his sister Gracie sat proudly at the front row, gesticulating encouragement. The third lady accompanying him was his girlfriend Debbie. The locals had not been expecting a Zambian/English presence that evening, but she certainly made the occasion all the more glamorous. Behind her sat the fourth and fifth females to escort Sean – Merle and Olivia. They were good friends who were on their first visit to Ireland, and they could not believe that their male host was now a celebrity! Merle

Willis was Debbie's younger step-sister. Aged 20, she was Caucasian, and wore a short tomboyish hairstyle. Her giggly friend with long natural blonde curls was Olivia Sheldon-Lovett. They were both students in the Arts faculty of the prestigious Sorbonne University in Paris. And were on a long-arranged four night break to stay with Debbie in Dublin. Little had they realised that they would end up spending two of those nights in North West Mayo, but the experience greatly enriched their trip.

They joined in the clapping as Sean, after receiving accolades for 'his poetic talent', stepped to the microphone stand and accepted his prizes. He became emotional as he spoke of his December visit to the town and paid tribute to Umberto and Deirdre who were present. Camera bulbs flashed as he posed with the judges of the competition, but his happiest moment came when he had a photograph taken with 'his' five women. He even signed some autographs for local school children who brought printed copies of 'Erris-istible' along to the ceremony. After being thanked for applying his talents to the cause of tourism in North West Mayo, Sean treated the five females and himself to a tasty meal in The Anchor Hotel out of his winnings. He was in jovial form, and downed several glasses of wine before he, Debbie, Merle and Olivia took to their cosy beds in the 'High Drift' Bed and Breakfast on the Ballina Road, where they were treated like royalty.

Mrs and Ms McRobert returned to Castlebar by car – with the trophy. Peter McRobert had decided not to travel to the award ceremony. He feigned a reason not to attend, but in reality he was suspicious about his son's achievement. He wondered to himself how his son had all of a sudden become an acclaimed poet when there had been no previous indicators of this talent. And he wondered how come his son was now an apparent expert on a corner of Mayo that he had barely visited. But he would keep his lip buttoned – for the time being at least.

Erris-istible

You might find your heaven by Broadhaven's Stacks,
And th'Atlantic's aroma might help you relax.
You might find Bangor's village a joy to behold,
But the secret that's Erris is yet to be told.
You might gaze on ghosts in Belmullet's Square,
Of souls still enjoying their An Leabha Fair,
The Devil may tempt you but you'll be swayed by God,
Who'll assuage your stresses with views of Blacksod.
Doohoma's idyllic and Geesala's like home,
It feels like you'll need no longer to roam,
Mountjubilee glistens gloriously nearby,
And in the distance you can see Ballycroy.
The hills and the heather; the inlets and lake,
Invaders tried theft here but they failed to take.
Others sought refuge and won warm embraces,
And they got to gallop Doolough's Great Races.
The sun sets here but many sons sail,
Along with their sisters a troublesome trail,
But when their eyes rest 'neath faraway beams,
They revisit Erris in their homecoming dreams.
Oh you kind folk of Erris how blessed are ye,
To've been sprinkled with Islands like dear Inishkea,
I envy your Inver, I covet Glenamoy,
I'd love to be buried in Old Ballinaboy.
Oh look there at Achill, and at that pyramid rock,
That rises from the ocean – the pirates to block,
Strands that stretch forever for the youngsters to run,
And the gold that's created by the rays of the sun.
There's many a headstone and many a cross,
Symbols of hardship, of victory and loss.
But though they now lie 'neath sacred ground,
Blessed are those who this corner found.
You might forget that there is - another place,
Where you must return to – to rejoin the race,
You might forget this is just a haven for me and for you,
But its kind dwellers are indeed God's chosen few.
So I leave Irresistible Erris in North West Mayo,
Back to the grey city now I must go,
But my heart it's much warmer and my mind now clear,
And I pray God rewards me a return next year.

Saturday 1st March 1997

The foursome enjoyed a scrumptious breakfast in the friendly
B&B. They were delighted to see that it was a mild morning, with
the sun trying to break through the clouds. They were having
good fun as a group. Debbie was glad to catch up with her step
sister, and Olivia was giddy with excitement to find herself away
from the city of Paris and in this sanctuary by the shores of the
Atlantic. Debbie had brought her company car, and as they were
waved away from Belmullet Sean sat in the passenger seat giving
directions. They had made a booking to stay in another B&B on
Saturday night, this time on Achill Island. Although less than 10
miles away 'as the crow flies' they had a 40 mile journey in front
of them. But they were in no hurry.

On learning that she was visiting this corner of Connaught for the
prize-giving ceremony, Merle had asked to take advantage of the
trip so as to visit the Art Centre on Achill Island established by
her favourite German writer Heinrich Böll. He and his wife had
lived on the idyllic island for many years. Merle was fascinated by
his work and life story, and could not pass up on such an
opportunity. Luckily her sister, her sister's boyfriend and her best
friend were agreeable to the trip. The only thing that began to
annoy Debbie as she steered her car southwards was the fact that
Olivia kept asking her to stop the car because she wanted to take
so many photographs of the scenery. The bogland and forestry
fascinated her, as did the sheep grazing by the roadside! She had
never seen anything like this before, and was using up an
incredible amount of film. Sensing her annoyance, Sean consoled
Debbie with an odd kiss on her cheek and a regular rub of her
shapely thigh.

He formed a good relationship with Merle and Olivia, and there
was much banter between them all. Merle noticed that Sean was
not her step-sister's 'usual type' but she appeared happy with him
and that was the main thing. And Debbie WAS happy. Despite
her misgivings at Christmas, she had observed a more vulnerable
side to Sean after the death of Teeko. She felt that she could not
abandon him in his hour of need. His sadness over losing his best

143

friend bonded the couple closer together. She loved his new long hairstyle with it's dangly locks that seemed to make his eyes more mischievous. And she loved his trim firm body. She was glad that he was showing a healthy interest in his temporary catering job and contemplating pursuing that as an alternative career. She was proud that he had won the award, and that he was making a real effort with his writing. He had signed up with a writers agency in Dublin. He had submitted 'his' finalised novel to several publishing houses. He had submitted some songs and poems to recording artists. He made her feel comfortable and wanted. He showered gifts upon her. Yes, she was happy.

Sean was happy too as he thought of what he might do with the remainder of his £1,000 prize. He was footing the bill for all food, drink and accommodation costs for the weekend – something that really impressed the students! Something that impressed Sean was the fact that Olivia's father owned a publishing company in England, Ellisel Publishing Limited. She promised to bring back copies of Sean's work for him to assess.

As they took a right turn at Bangor Erris towards Ballycroy, Sean was deep in thought. He had successfully used the five women to distract himself and to fend off upset on revisiting the site of Teeko's death. Yet, he still missed his lanky, funny looking 'spud-head' of a pal. He was also thinking of Thomas, whose home parish he was now about to enter for the first time since his funeral. He knew deep down that he was a fraud. He knew deep down that he was wrongly benefiting from Thomas's talents. He knew deep down that he would not have ever met Debbie if he had not met Thomas. He knew deep down that some day this would all catch up on him. He knew deep down that he would continue to have regular ghostly visits from Mary Beth. But for now, a lot of things were going his way. Ever since he met Thomas, he felt invigorated. It felt as if a new, stronger engine of life was pumping the blood through his veins. He felt inspired. He felt confident. He felt assured. He knew he was giving off very positive vibes. Beauties like Debbie would never have given 'the old Sean' a second glance. He knew he felt guilty, but "what the hell - Thomas is being portrayed as a saint when I know the reality: that he was not only two-timing Ursula but four-timing her! He was smart. He was clever. He was handsome. He was talented. He was well liked. But he was no saint!"

Olivia asked Debbie to stop her sleek black Toyota car again as she was struck by the sight of Slieve Mór appearing in front of them as they neared Ballycroy. The giant triangle of a mountain certainly cut an impressive image, as the straight narrow road ahead with tall gracious green pines on either side made a picture postcard scene.
"Wow" said Olivia "That's awesome! Like a giant shark fin jutting out of the water!"
"That's part of Achill Island, we will be there in a couple of hours" said Sean.
"A couple of hours?!" squeaked Debbie. "Surely it won't take us that long?!"
"Well, we will have a stop in Ballycroy" replied Sean. "There is only one pub in the place, and it's supposed to have the best pint of Guinness in Ireland. So we shall sample that!" His proposition received a 'hurrah' from the two girls in the rear seat.

But before they reached the terminus for their thirst, a patient Debbie had to stop the car a couple of more times as Olivia captured pictures of the flowing Shranamonragh River and Bunmore Hill. The arrival of three attractive young ladies certainly brightened up the day for the regulars in Cleary's Bar. Not much notice was taken of their male companion! Debbie, Merle and Olivia were as amazed as the locals – but for different reasons:
"Wow, this is like going back in time!" said the open mouthed Olivia. "I love this place, I absolutely love it!"
The stone floor, the old wooden panelling, the stained old photographs, the absence of music, the friendly attentive staff – it all contributed to an old style ambiance. There was an easy-going atmosphere, no one was rushing, the drinkers were savouring every mouthful and rays of the sun came through the windows to light up the dated décor. Old bottles and jugs from over 50 years previously sat on the shelves above the new alco-pops and bottled beer. None of the four had ever before seen a bar counter continue in through a wall and become a shop counter in an adjoining room of the same building.

"This is amazing!" repeated Olivia. "You could get your shopping done while you get drunk!"

"Brilliant!" replied Sean. "And the Guinness is even better than I could have imagined!"

"Here's to Belmullet, Ballycroy and Achill!" toasted Debbie and they all joined in.

"And here's to the great poet Sean McRobert!" toasted Merle. "He is a poet – and he doesn't even know it!"

As Sean swallowed another mouthful of frothy Guinness, he thought of Thomas Goy lying in his grave just a couple of hundred yards away. He momentarily considered visiting the grave, but he thought it may put a dampener on their day. In any case, he would not risk leaving his three women alone in the pub because by the way the local admirers were advancing into their circle; there was a good chance that the three of them might have been the recipients of marriage proposals by the time he returned! And maybe all three women would have been tempted by life as a farmer's wife in this peaceful part of the world!

By 3pm the black Toyota was weaving it's away along the winding road from Ballycroy to Mulranny on the way to Achill. With a steep mountain range on the left and calm mirror-like inlet waters to the right, Olivia continued to hinder the journey with her photographic requests. She promised to return some day with her own car and an even better camera – one that would do justice to the panoramic portraits that were being presented to her.

The fulfilled foursome spent a heavenly night on Ireland's largest island, as the frothy waves from the Atlantic Ocean crashed off the nearby granite cliffs. As they drifted off to sleep, each of them promised themselves that they would return another day.

"Your next poem will have to be about Achill" said Debbie just before she kissed her boyfriend good night.

"No my next poem will be about YOU!" smiled Sean from his cosy pillow. But the reality was that he did not have the talent to compose a poem or a song that could capture her beauty.

Nevertheless, little did he know that on that very same evening, an up-and-coming American group called 'Urban Spice' had recorded one of 'his' ditties in a Brooklyn studio. A poem that Thomas Goy had scrawled had now been transformed into a rap offering – and would feature in one of the best selling American albums of 1997. Before submitting it through the Dublin-based agency that represented him, Sean had adjusted some of the original lyrics. He added the 'pony-tail' line as a nod to the 'gossip-columnist', even though the composition seemed to be about a female. Little did he know that wads of royalty payments would soon be en-route to add to his stash of ill-gotten gains. The man of fraud was about to enter another stratosphere...

Silly Silly Writer

Silly Silly Writer,
If Only she'd been Brighter,
She wouldn't be a Dog,
And I wouldn't have to Bite her.
If only She'd been Smart,
And shown a bit of Heart,
She wouldn't be a Donkey,
And Pulling you – her Cart.
Silly Silly Writer,
Your Page it should be Whiter,
Don't Spoil it with your Ink,
And your Deadlines might get Tighter.
If only you'd a Brain,
A Thought or two you'd Gain,
But now it's much Too Late,
So Away with you Again.
Silly Silly Writer,
How I'd Love to Fight her,
And Snip that Pony Tail,
To Make the Burden Lighter.

CHAPTER 27
Thursday 9th September 1999

A proud Sean McRobert stood in front of the full length mirror. He was admiring himself, on this, the most special of days. His wedding day. The ninth of the ninth nineteen ninety nine!

He admired his long brown hair, parted in the middle, which rested neatly on his shoulders. He admired his thin chiselled face. He admired his smig. He admired the three piece morning suit that he wore. He admired the shine that came from his £1,000 shoes. He looked around. He admired the wonderful antique furniture of the classically decorated room in which he had just spent his last night as a single man. It was a room in Cooling Castle, Kent, England which his father-in-law to-be had hired for three days and three nights to celebrate the much anticipated wedding. The saffron September sun lit up the room as the grandfather clock ticked towards noon.

There was a lot going through the mind of the groom that day. He had a lot to think about. How would his bride-to-be be feeling at this very moment? Did his parents and sister enjoy their first night in the castle? Did his best man have the rings? Would the speech be alright? Would there be any trouble at the wedding?

Wouldn't it have been nice if Teeko had lived to see this day? And if his grandfather had lived to see it too? Wouldn't Thomas be proud of him?

He smiled as he thought about the contract with 'Hello' magazine that was essentially paying for the wedding and the luxurious honeymoon in Mauritius. He smiled as he thought of the size of his bank balance. He smiled as he thought of the money that was snowballing its way to him in royalty payments. He smiled as he remembered the forlorn days when he was a struggling student. He smiled as he remembered the women he had slept with – conquests who would no doubt find today a bitter experience as he wedded his ultimate choice. He smiled as he remembered the cream coloured Mercedes-Benz and its smiling steerer slowing down to pick him up almost three years earlier – the moment that changed his life forever.

His thoughts were disrupted by the entrance of his Best Man Ralph into the room.
"You are ready already!" exclaimed the posh English accent. "My goodness. You ARE eager, aren't you my good friend?"
"Mad for road!" replied Sean laughing. "Did you see any of my crew yet?"
"Yes indeed, your parents and delightful sister are dining as we speak. They are immensely proud of you, you know. Jolly good breakfast they serve here too" said Ralph. "Any sign of His Lordship?"
"Not yet!" answered Sean. "But I hope the fecker has calmed down after yesterday. I know he's paying for all of this but he better not spoil our day!"

'His Lordship' was the father of the bride-to-be, and several minutes later he stormed into Sean's bedroom, signalling that he was still in atrocious form:
"I ask you to do ONE thing and you cannot do it! Just ONE thing!" roared the burley Briton.
"What IS the matter, Sir?" asked Ralph.
"I will tell you what the matter is, shall I? The matter is – that that Irish Imbecile I asked to keep away from this forsaken castle is right outside the gate. Yes. There he is. With his placard as usual. Splendid. Just splendid! Did I NOT ask that you ensure that he is kept away – just for ONE day?!! Did I NOT ask that?!
"I will see to it that he disappears, Sir" said Ralph, rushing out of the oak panelled room.
"You DO that!" was the yelled reply in a harsh tone. "If that imbecile spoils my daughter's wedding day then you shall pay dearly, Ralph! Do NOT let me down today of ALL days!"

The man scurrying towards the castle entrance was a tall, thin, flame haired, Old Etonian named Ralph Ramsbottom. His profession was that of Personal Assistant to Sean McRobert, now world renowned as S.R.McRobert, the famous novelist.

The man holding a placard of protest at the castle gates was the bane of his life. His name was Norman O'Toole. The lanky, painfully thin ex-psychiatric patient, with the huge forehead. The man from Kerry, who had been a housemate of Thomas Goy at the time of his death.

For almost two years now, Norman had been dedicating his life to attempting to highlight to the world that the acclaimed author S.R.McRobert was indeed 'a fraud'. The emaciated 'Irish Imbecile' would turn up at book launches and speaking events – basically wherever Sean was making a public appearance. Ever since recognising him once his photograph started appearing in the newspapers for the success of the song 'Silly Writer' and the novel 'The Mayo Ghost Story' Norman embarked on a quest for justice. He told anyone who dared to listen that the Mayo man was a fake. He had stolen his material from a dead man. Not only that, he had stolen property from that same dead man. And Norman had ended up spending time incarcerated because he had been wrongly accused.

Physical threats and barring orders had not dissuaded the determined Norman from his campaign. He was determined to show up Sean for who and what he really was. A 'Cheat'. A 'Grave-robber'. A 'Fraudster'. A 'Con-artist'. A 'Liar'. All slogans that appeared on his hand-painted signs.

At stages Norman had roped in some supporters. Gordon, who spoke at Thomas's funeral, joined in at the start but quickly faded. Thomas's brother Anthony promised his support but he was fighting a battle with alcohol and the alcohol was winning. As many of the events Sean was appearing at were outside of Ireland, many potential co-protestors found the travel and accommodation costs prohibitive. Norman was resentful that his elderly father had gone to his grave thinking that Norman had been the robber. He was now using all of his late father's inheritance money to try and prove that the real culprit was the man now being acclaimed as Ireland's greatest contemporary literary talent. And protesting at his high-profile wedding was an opportunity that Norman could not afford to miss as he tried to maximise attention for his cause.

On 9/9/99, the threats of physicality turned to actual physicality as Ralph enlisted the help of the castle's security team to bundle the protestor into a jeep and ensure he was driven as far away from Kent as possible. Ralph was under orders to ensure that the paparazzi did not get any photographs of 'the snake in paradise'. Battered and bloodied, Norman was taken on a long tour of England's chalky south coast, as the guests started arriving for the matrimonial ceremony.

Just after noon, a proud Sean McRobert inhaled a deep breath as he laid eyes on his beautiful bride at the bottom of the aisle. Flanked by the faithful Ralph, he broke into a smile as the tones of 'Here Comes the Bride' floated through the air from the string quartet as his soon-to-be father-in-law forced a smile for the intimate contingent of fifty guests. Peter McRobert held the hand of his weeping wife Joan as their son exchanged vows with the English lady.

"Do you, Sean Robert McRobert, take Olivia Joyce Sheldon-Lovett to be your lawfully wedded wife?" asked the vicar.
"I do" replied Sean firmly.
"And do you, Olivia Joyce Sheldon-Lovett take Sean Robert McRobert to be your lawfully wedded husband?"
"I do!" replied the giggling bride, her blonde tresses falling from beneath her veil.

Within moments, the congregation clapped as the vicar pronounced them as 'Man and Wife'. The 'Hello' team of photographers then took control of proceedings, as everyone put on their best smiles to accompany their best outfits. Even Sir Lionel Sheldon-Lovett himself, the multi-millionaire owner of Ellisel Publishers Limited, managed a genuine smile as he posed with his only child and his new son-in-law.

Sean's parents and sister marvelled at the luxurious surroundings. It was another major milestone in their life. Sean had certainly come a long way from his days as a reluctant student boarding the bus from Castlebar to Dublin on Sunday evenings. The lad who never had much interest in reading or writing was now an acclaimed author! And the lad who never did put any energy into finding girlfriends had now hooked himself one of Britain's most eligible heiresses. Just by marrying her he had turned himself into a multi-millionaire, at the age of 23! And he was already well on the way to becoming a millionaire before that – thanks mainly to the incredible worldwide promotional machine that was Ellisel Publishing Ltd.

Peter McRobert still had strong doubts about the authenticity of his author son. He knew that it was more than a coincidence that his son had become an almost overnight sensation after the death of his writer friend. When he had confronted Sean with his suspicions, they had been firmly denied. And for the sake of keeping his loyal wife happy, Peter McRobert had gone along with supporting Sean's progress in his new career. But every night the devoted Roman Catholic prayed hard that his son would be guided along 'the right path' and be forgiven for any sins he had committed.

'The Mayo Ghost Story' had been adapted into localised versions to suit local markets, and was a phenomenal success in the English speaking world. For example, in America it was published as 'The Gainsville Ghost Story' and in England into 'The Gosforth Ghost Story'. Advance payments had already rolled in for TV and film rights. On top of this, 'Silly Writer' had brought in almost a quarter of a million pounds alone. S.R.McRobert had become an in-demand celebrity who could charge outrageous amounts in appearance fees. His romance with the photogenic Olivia, a regular on the Paris and London social scene, only served to increase his worth.

But every silver cloud, of course, has a dark lining and the continuing frequent visitations from Mary Beth formed part of that dark line. The protests of the wronged Norman formed another part of that dark line. And to complete it, Sean had just narrowly avoided litigation for fraud. His wealthy and influential father-in-law and backer had rescued him. Foolishly, on finding out in late 1997 that 'Die in Ohio' had been featured on the soundtrack of a successful American movie, Sean impersonated the late Thomas Goy in an attempt to secure increased royalties. A cheque from the USA was despatched for ten thousand dollars.

Sean amended the payee name, but his fraud was detected. He had to admit his misdemeanour to the irate Sir Lionel Sheldon-Lovett, who paid an even larger sum to appease the prosecutors. The incident planted the first seed of doubt in the old man's head that the naysayer Norman O'Toole might not have been 100% wrong.

But on this sunny September day, the wealthy businessman was determined to ensure that his daughter and heiress would enjoy a fairytale wedding that she would never forget. On Sean's side, only three were invited and only three attended the wedding. There was no Dexter, no Jamesie, no student friends, no ex-girlfriends. He was now in a separate successful social sphere.

He was also on his way to a honeymoon on the white sands of Mauritius and its turquoise waters, the island once described as 'the place God modelled paradise on'. By saying "I do" he had become part owner of properties in England, France, America, South Africa and Australia. With Olivia being an only child, Sean not only became a son-in-law to Sir Lionel Sheldon-Lovett, but a son. The personal wedding gift handed over on the eve of the wedding was a private jet! But the jet was just a symbol of the world of wealth that the young Mayo man was now stepping into.

Sean was fast leaving the ordinary Irish lifestyle behind him. Other than his parents and sister, and his late grandfather, he thanked no-one else from Ireland in his wedding speech. As the guests downed the finest champagne and caviar in toasting the happy couple, the rotting corpse of the unaccredited real author that had brought Sean to this point lay beneath the Ballycroy soil. An aggrieved Debbie Willis lay in the Majorca sun with her sister who –ridden with guilt for inadvertently introducing Olivia to Sean – had paid for a holiday to whisk her away from England whilst the wedding took place. In Dublin, genuine tears of torment flowed down the freckled cheeks of Sean's ex-girlfriend Yvonne. The heartbroken girl had read about the wedding plans in a magazine article. It was a horrible day for her to endure.

Only late in the evening of his wedding, as he emptied his bladder up against a gold coloured urinal, did a pang of guilt hit the

153

drunken Sean as he recalled the parts played and paid by the late Thomas Goy in his good fortune. "Why doesn't he come back to haunt me?" Sean asked himself. "If a wee thing like Mary Beth can try to take me over from the beyond, why doesn't a big man like him try? He MUST be angry with me! Why, look at all of this, this luxury. I would not be here but for him. Through him I met Debbie and through Debbie I met my wife. Oh Thomas, when will you reap your vengeance against me? WHEN?"

As he staggered from the male toilet, Sean sang a verse from one of the Depeche Mode tunes from the CD he had stolen from Thomas's home:

"Tonight, I'm in the hands of fate, I hand myself over on a plate!" he laughed as Ralph intervened to lead the groom to the castle's honeymoon suite. Sean was in no state to consummate the marriage on his wedding night, but he had ample time for that on the upcoming luxurious sun-soaked honeymoon.

The date of 9/9/99 had been hastily chosen as a wedding date as it was considered a lucky day to tie the knot. Hundreds of couples around the world had picked that date for the same reason. Only time would tell if the luck of Sean McRobert would continue to hold out...

CHAPTER 28

Friday 1st September 2006

The staff in the Garda Headquarters in The Phoenix Park in Dublin Ireland were giddy with excitement. Particularly the young secretarial staff. Today was the date that the force's newest and youngest Chief Superintendent was taking up his post. He had shot like a rocket up through the Garda ranks, and his high-profile success in securing a casualty-free outcome to a much publicised Irish kidnapping case had made him a household name. His rugged but handsome features, tall strong physique and charming ways with the media had given him virtually celebrity status. He eagerly looked forward to his new promoted assignment.

Chief Superintendent Daithí 'Dashing' Donaghy smiled as he was introduced to his new colleagues, and shown to his immaculately decorated office. He was 30 years of age and married to a barrister. They had two small children. His nose was still a bit crooked from his boxing days, but he had a head full of dark hair with not a grey rib in sight, and he still had his shiny white teeth. One could only be impressed whenever this fine specimen in uniform appeared. He was the pride of Belmullet.

As he settled into his swivel chair and placed a photograph of his wife and children on his desk, he knew that today would be an 'easing-in' day and that a relaxing weekend lay ahead. It was supposed to be good luck to start a new job on a Friday. The real work would start on Monday morning. But there was one file he wanted to see, and it was the first request he made of the secretary assigned to him.

"Can you bring me the file on Sean Robert McRobert please?" he asked gently, sensing the nervousness of the young female.
"Of course Chief Superintendent" she replied. "Are you sure you won't have a tea or a coffee?"
"Never touch the stuff!" he smiled. "So you won't have to worry about me on that score. The joke in my last place was that I could not handle anything hot!" to which the secretary giggled.

Before long, Daithí was eagerly reading through the file of his fellow Mayoman. Being so busy himself, he had lost track of recent events surrounding the mystifying man from Castlebar he had first met some ten years earlier. He read through the bulky file from cover to cover:

First came to Garda attention in a brawl in Newport in 1996. Was present at the death of Sean 'Teeko' Murphy in Belmullet – also in 1996. Then came under scrutiny as an acquaintance of Simon 'Chucky' English in Dublin's north inner city. Then became the subject of an accusation of impersonation and theft lodged by Norman O'Toole in 1997. Left his college studies and appeared in Brighton in the United Kingdom as a published author. Had worldwide success with the book 'The Mayo Ghost Story' and the song 'Silly Writer'. Estimated to be a millionaire by 1998. Accused of fraud by the CIA over the rights to the song "Die in Ohio" but charges were dropped. Took out a barring order against Norman O'Toole and sued him for slander. Married the wealthy heiress Olivia Sheldon-Lovett in 1999. Arrested in Hove near Brighton in 2000 and extradited to Ireland, where he was placed on trial for conspiracy to murder Norman O'Toole. He was found guilty of offering Simon 'Chucky' English £50,000 to kill Norman O'Toole. Instead of 'taking out' McRobert's nemesis Norman, Chucky went straight to the authorities. Sentenced to ten years imprisonment in Mountjoy Prison. Sales of his book rocketed. In 2003 he was divorced by Olivia Sheldon-Lovett. He is believed to have received a settlement in the region of £20 million. Appealed his conviction in 2004 and was granted compassionate release to attend the funeral of his father in Castlebar. In late 2005 his conviction was quashed as the Supreme Court decided that the testimony of Chucky was unreliable. Has sued the state and is line for compensation of at least €2 million. Is now living in Reigate, Surrey, UK, with his new fiancée Yvonne Griffin – his former girlfriend from college – who began visiting him in Mountjoy in 2004.

"Wow!" sighed Daithí as he sat back on his comfortable chair. "Hasn't that man lived a charmed life?! They fete ME as being successful, but I don't have millions in MY bank account!"

He called in his secretary, and asked her to send in Sergeant Hayden, who he understood to be the HQ's 'expert' on McRobert.

"I believe you were once a friend of McRobert, Sir?" enquired the moustachioed Sergeant Hayden.

"Would you believe, he attended my 21st birthday party many moons ago?!" laughed Daithí.

"Really!" responded Hayden. "Guilty by association, Sir?!"

"Guilty of not spotting a master fraudster and schemer!" replied Daithí with a smile. "But, he is now a free man and has probably more money than the entire Garda force of Ireland will earn this year! So who is the fool?"

"He definitely sought to have that Kerry fellow Norman whacked" stated the Sergeant. "I still don't know how he got the whole thing quashed. And the state will be broke from the compensation bill."

"I know" replied Daithí solemnly. "But actually, it's hard for me to say this, but he wasn't a bad fellow! I mean – he was devious and clever but he wasn't naturally a man of malice."

"Ah come on now Chief Inspector" piped up Sergeant Hayden. "Norman O'Toole is lucky to be alive. If Chucky had taken the money and seen the job through McRobert would be a murderer!"

"I know, I know" replied Daithí. "But you know what I mean. He is not the born scum element we deal with everyday. He just got greedy and fell into that trap."

"A crime is a crime is a crime, Sir" stated Hayden.

"You don't have to tell ME that!" said Daithí sternly, "But I still think McRobert is a fascinating character. You know, they say he did not write those books or songs at all, that he stole them from Norman's housemate! A man named Thomas Goy."

"I am well aware of that" said Hayden. "But he is supposed to be releasing his life story soon, which will probably make a few more million. He is supposed to have started it in The Joy. So he must have SOME writing capability!"

"Sure even the caddie picks up some good shots from observing the pro" said Daithí using his golfing analogy. "From copying all of those scripts he must have picked up a few tips. Imagine, if Goy had lived, how successful he would have been. And do you know that I met him in my youth too?"

"Really?!" answered Hayden impressed. "YOU should write the book. It might top-up your pension, Sir!"

"So, Sergeant Hayden, as you are the 'McRobert Expert' around here I will hand this file back to you. Where is he now? Living in Surrey still?" asked Daithí.
"Would you believe he is actually in Ireland right now. He is actually in YOUR county TODAY!" replied Hayden.
"Mayo?! What's he doing there? Visiting his mother and sister in Castlebar?" enquired a surprised Daithí.
"Perhaps. But he is honeymooning there. In the Westport and Achill region, they tell me. He and his long-lost love Yvonne got married here in Dublin during the week! A Registry Office job!" came the reply.
"Are you serious?" asked Daithí.
"Deadly!" retorted Hayden. "Both now on their second marriages. But no kids. And all of the money in the world and where do they go on honeymoon – bloody Mayo!"
"Now now, Sergeant Hayden!" responded Daithí semi-seriously, leaning across the table. "I will not hear a bad word about my native county! Retract that immediately and you might be lucky to get some leave next year – which you MUST spend in Mayo!"
"I retract! Sorry Sir!" smiled the sergeant, raising from his seat and grabbing the file to take out of the office with him. "It is a wonder you were not invited to the wedding, Sir, being a friend of his and all that?"
"Oh, the less weddings I am invited to the better!" replied Daithí. "And anyway I think someone from 'the law' is the last person McRobert would want to see on his big day! Thanks Sergeant Hayden, and enjoy your weekend."
"You too, Sir" was the answer "And good luck to Mayo in the final in a fortnight. I hope ye do it THIS time!"
"I hope so too!" smiled the Chief Inspector.

As the staff of Garda HQ and the rest of professional Dublin geared themselves for a weekend break, the city prepared to lose half its population that sunny September evening, despite the fact that thousands of hurling fans were due in Croke Park for the All Ireland hurling final.

Down in Ballycroy's hillside graveyard, under the shadow of Bunmore Hill, the only crowding visible was the tightly placed array of headstones, as the rays of the sun bounced off the shiny marble. At 5pm, only one living person was present within the walled resting-place for the parish's deceased. Tears fell from the eyes of the now-muscular ex-convict who stared at the headstone of Thomas Goy, now almost a decade dead.

"I am so sorry, Thomas, I really am!" he cried. "I am sorry for taking from you. I am sorry about Ursula. I am sorry about your poor family. I am sorry about your friend Norman. I am sorry about your three women in Dublin. I am really really sorry Thomas. I am sorry I brought you such bad luck that evening. You should be alive now, married with children, and earning from your writing. I am sorry I have stolen your life!"

This outpouring surprised even Sean McRobert himself. In his lowest moments in prison, he had promised that he would visit the grave of his hero and lay flowers there when he was out. Earlier that week, as he prepared for his pilgrimage, he had anonymously posted thousands of euros in an effort to alleviate his guilt. He had posted €1,000 to the local GAA club. Another €1,000 to the local church. And finally €10,000 in a package simply addressed Anthony Goy, Ballycroy – the only sibling of Thomas. It was 'guilt money' – but he hoped it would help in some way and make the spirit of Thomas happy.

"Why haven't you haunted me? Why?" the new groom exclaimed as his wails echoed off the erect headstones. "Why do you never haunt me like SHE does? Why don't you ever appear in my dreams anymore? It has been YEARS! I NEED to know if you're angry with me? I NEED to know, Thomas, PLEASE!! I remember what you said ten years ago about not just getting even but getting ahead and what revenge you are capable of. WHERE is your revenge on ME? Was it losing Teeko? Was it losing Dad? Was it losing Grand-dad? Is it my mother's illness? Is it Gracie's miscarriages? Was it prison? Was it my divorce? Why don't you just appear in a dream? WHY Thomas, WHY don't you? Just send me a sign, PLEASE! I dream of Dad, Grand-dad, Teeko, Norman, Chucky, Olivia, sheep, cows, dogs, cars, Prison Officers – EVERYTHING except the fucking thing I want to dream about

– YOU! SHE still comes on me – 'Mary Beth' – but every time that chilly feeling comes upon me I pray that it is YOU. Is SHE your messenger, Thomas? Is she your vessel? I am going MAD here, Thomas, PLEASE send me a sign. I NEED to know if you are happy that I have brought your work to the wide world. I NEED to know what you think. Or I will go MAD! PLEASE?!!"

Sean's shadow led him towards his Land Cruiser as he left the cemetery. He had fulfilled his promise to visit Thomas's grave. But he had not yet the answer he craved. He admired the brown, gold and green scenery as the solar rays lit up the picturesque parish on his drive back to the Mulranny Hotel where his new bride Yvonne was being treated to a heavenly massage. This very landscape had inspired the person he had stolen from. Tears continued to roll down the cheeks of the balding multi-millionaire as he left Ballycroy behind.

The tenth anniversary of Thomas's passing was only four weeks away. But Sean felt as close to him as he had done on that fateful October evening. Unbelievably, as Sean switched on the vehicle's radio as he neared Mulranny, the song that was playing was Bob Dylan's angry anthem 'Positively 4th Street' that Goy had introduced to him:
"You gotta lot a nerve, to say you are my friend,
When I was down you just stood there grinning,
You gotta lot of nerve, to say you have a helping hand to give,
You just wanna be on the side that's winning!"

Was this a cryptic sign from the Ballycroy crypt?

CHAPTER 29

Friday 10th May 2013

Assistant Commissioner Daithí Donaghy had a few hours to kill. The conference on international crime that he had attended in the heart of London had ended earlier than expected. Most of the conference delegates capitalised on this time by doing some shopping on Bond Street and Leicester Square. But the head of the Irish delegation had other ideas. He would call in on an old friend!

The successful Sean McRobert and his wife and child lived in the affluent old English town of Reigate, several miles from London's Gatwick Airport, from where Daithí was due to fly back from later that evening. It didn't take much of Daithí's detective skills to locate the McRobert mansion on the outskirts of Reigate. The black London taxi was granted access to the grounds by the resident servant Morgan. The elderly butler led Daithí in through the front door as the taxi left the estate, with an order to return in an hour and bring the elite policeman to the airport.

Sean was surprised when his distinguished visitor was announced, and although he was not entirely in the mood for a visitor – especially a senior policeman – he felt he had little option but to welcome his guest from the same western county as he himself hailed from.

Daithí surveyed the magnificent furniture and décor as he waited for Sean to arrive in the sitting room. He could smell the scent of pound notes dripping from every picture frame, candelabra and chandelier. He admired the bronze figurines and the velvety purple curtains. The carpet felt like a sponge beneath his shiny shoes. He caught a glimpse of himself in an ornately framed mirror and tried to put an estimate on the costs of the grand piano, cello and antique gramophone that took pride of place. He looked at the expensive red armchairs and wondered if he might fall asleep should he sit in one, they looked so welcoming. His thoughts were interrupted by the arrival of his reluctant host.

"DASHING Daithí Donaghy!" came the familiar voice. "Well, I never! NOW you visit me! Where were you when I pined for visitors in The Joy – and you just stationed down the road from me?!"

"Still the sense of humour!" laughed Daithí. "Good to see you, Mister McRobert!"

The men shook hands firmly and took a comfortable seat each, as Sean instructed Morgan to bring them each a glass of brandy.

"Still as dashing as ever, I see!" laughed Sean.

"None of that stuff now!" chuckled Daithí. "Don't make me feel uncomfortable. I know what prison can do to a man!"

Sean laughed wholeheartedly and rubbed his hands through the few strands of hair that remained on his scalp.

"Anyway" continued the senior Garda, "Sure a visit to one of Ireland's top criminals would not have been ideal for my CV. I couldn't be seen visiting you – even though I wanted to!"

"I suppose! You are excused so!" replied a jovial Sean.

"And in any case, I doubt a visit from a top cop would have won you any brownie-points from your fellow inmates!" added Daithí.

"True!" replied Sean laughing. "So, 'Mister Belmullet-Man-Makes-It-Good', to what do I now owe the privilege of your presence?"

"YOU are the successful one, look at this palace!" said Daithí, looking around the room. "Crime certainly pays!"

"Whoah! Hold on there, hold on!" interrupted Sean, smirking. "Everything has been quashed. You cannot say that, Daithí! I am innocent of ALL charges!"

"You are indeed!" responded Daithí. "But we have a nice thick file on you all the same. And normally there is no need to set up a file on the son of an ordinary Agricultural Inspector from Mayo!"

The banter continued for quite a while and it was clear that there was an element of mutual respect between the two acquaintances from Mayo. Their career paths had diverged, but they updated each other on whatever mutual friends they could think of.

Sean told how he was happier now than he ever had been. His six year old daughter was upstairs playing but his wife was away for the afternoon. He had chosen to live close to Gatwick Airport as he still had his private jet, and he regularly needed to fly to book-related events all over the world. His autobiography "How Wronged Was I?" and his own work of 'fiction' "Don't Just Get Even – Get Ahead" had been massive global successes and had further stacked up the cash in his numerous offshore bank accounts.

Daithí felt boring in comparison when he spoke of his climb to the rank of Assistant Commissioner – Ireland's youngest. In typical policeman fashion, he kept focusing the 'spotlight' on the person that sat across from him and felt at ease interrogating instead of being interrogated. He told his host that he visited because he genuinely believed that Sean was not a natural criminal, but simply someone normal who got washed away on a tide of greed and materialism. An opportunist more than a plotter. A chancer more than a charger. The author listened with interest.

When Sean again began asking questions about Daithí's private life, the policeman rose from the cushioned comfort of his chair and began enquiring about the many pictures in the room.
"This must be your daughter, she is the image of you!" he said.
"Yes, that's Admira" replied the proud father.
"Six you say?"
"Yes, she is six. And spoilt!" laughed Sean.
"Admira, that's a nice name" said Daithí. "We have continued the trend of Irish names. Niamh is four and Oisín is two."
"Nice names too" said Sean. "The name 'Admira' came from the war in Serbia, Yvonne suggested it and I went with it."
"The war in Serbia, how do you mean?" enquired the tall Daithí as he looked at photos of weddings and other family events.
"She is named after Admira, who was a Bosnian Muslim who was trying to leave the city of Sarajevo with her boyfriend Bosko, a Bosnian Serb, in 1991 I think."
"Go on..." said Daithí as if he was interviewing a suspect.
"Well, both sides in the conflict had agreed a safe passage for the couple out of the city. But when they were crossing the bridge, a rogue sniper fired a shot and they both died, side by side."
"The one shot killed them both?!" queried Daithí.

"Apparently", said Sean, "But folklore says that it was he alone who was hit, and that Admira simply died beside him from a broken heart. Well, that's what Yvonne says anyway!"

"Amazing story! I must google that!" said Daithí.

"Far from bloody google you were reared!" laughed Sean. "Haven't you come a long way from good old Belmullet?! And by the way, how is my Italian friend Umberto?!"

Just as the black taxi arrived, little Admira appeared, fresh from playing with her dolls in her bedroom. Daithí admired her long brown hair and remarked on how beautiful she looked.

"I thought you said she looked like ME!" joked Sean.

"Very pleased to meet you" said the sweet English accent as she shook the hand of the imposing visitor.

"I have a small girl at home like you. She would LOVE to play with you, Admira!" said Daithí, kneeling.

"What is her name?" asked Admira.

"Niamh" answered Daithí. She has lovely long hair like you, and I have presents to bring her and her little monkey of a brother tonight." Then he turned to Sean.

"Gosh I'm sorry. I am the world's worst. I should have brought Admira something."

"Don't be silly!" insisted the little girl's father. "She has more than enough toys and books."

"What age is Niamh?" asked Admira, very mannerly.

"Four. And what age are you, Admira?"

"I am six!" she smiled. "And I will be seven in November. I cannot wait to be seven!"

"I bet you can't, seven is a great age! You will be a BIG girl then, won't you?" exclaimed Daithí, rising to his feet as the taxi driver blew a horn outside.

"I will. And what is the name of your monkey?" she asked innocently, thinking Niamh had a pet in Ireland.

"Oh he is only two. But he is a handful!" laughed Daithí.

In true West of Ireland fashion a minor scuffle broke out as the departing Daithí insisted on giving a £20 note to Admira. Sean physically resisting of course. The taller and stronger of the two managed to have his way, and apologised again for not bringing a toy for the little girl.

"I will buy something for my birthday with this. I shall put it in my piggy bank. Thank you sir" said Admira as she gave a hug to an impressed Daithí, who was feeling slightly choked as he thought of his evening reunion with his own little family back in Dublin.

The two men again firmly shook hands in front of Admira, Morgan and the cab driver as they prepared to part company. They wished each other well, and joked that they should meet at the Leabha Fair in Belmullet some August.
"I have one last thing to ask" said Daithí as he stood by the taxi door, which Morgan was holding open.
"Go on 'Columbo'!" laughed Sean "Out with it. Typical cop!"
"That poltergeist that visited you – Mary Beth – that you mention in your autobiography, does she still trouble you?" asked Daithí.
"Not for some years, Thank God!" said the author. "I think she got fed up of me. Yvonne credits my yoga regime!"
"Good for you!" said Daithí. "I really felt for you reading about that. Just READING about her attacking you like that sent shivers up MY spine. God only knows how YOU felt. Scary stuff!"
"Scary stuff indeed! It's not nice to be haunted!" replied Sean. "Listen. You take care of yourself and that family of yours, OK?"
"You too! Keep out of trouble and mind the three of you. Give my regards to your wife. It was good seeing you again" said Daithí as he took his rear seat. He proceeded to roll down the window and gesture goodbye to the waving Admira and the servant Morgan, and off he was whisked towards Gatwick.

As Daithí looked forward to seeing his family in Dublin within a couple of hours, he congratulated himself on making the effort to see his old friend. He was genuinely glad to see that Sean seemed at ease with himself. He was glad that he was well settled with two great girls in his life – AND a servant.

The visit had also made Sean feel good. He felt closer to home. It had been a huge gesture by Daithí, a kind of verification of his welcome back into the law-abiding world. A kind of acknowledgement that the past was over and forgotten about.

But was it over and forgotten about?

CHAPTER 30
Friday 4th October 2013

It was a calm but overcast day in Reigate in the South East of England. A thick layer of cloud prevented the sun from breaking through. But at least it was dry, and that allowed the landscaper to come and continue some of the work around the McRobert mansion, work that he had commenced some weeks earlier. It was Yvonne who was issuing the instructions to him. Sean wanted to focus on his latest book, and he took little notice of the comings and goings of the red Ford Transit van that Morgan let in and out of the estate.

"I am so excited, Daddy!" yelled Admira as she modelled her newest outfit. Her father admired her new overcoat, boots and beret as she danced excitedly waiting for Morgan to drive her and her mother to the airport. The family butler was being granted the rest of the afternoon off once he had completed his task.
"I can't wait to give Grandpa the present I got for him!" she exclaimed.
"He will love it I'm sure, Admira" said Sean, as his wife came down the stairs – also sporting a new coat and boots!
"Harrods did well on you two this week, I see!" smiled Sean.
"It's not often I get to splash out, Love!" replied his grinning wife, tongue firmly in cheek.
"Yeah, right!" responded Sean.

The writer was about to be treated to a rare weekend by himself. Morgan was taking a long weekend off. Yvonne and her daughter were flying in the private jet to Dublin, where they would celebrate the 70th birthday of Yvonne's father. Sean had opted not to attend, not that he was invited. Yvonne's parents had never quite forgiven him for the way he dumped their daughter back in their college days. He had betrayed the family trust. They had watched for years as she struggled to recover from losing 'the love of her life', and flitted from one disastrous relationship to another, culminating in an ill-advised marriage that predictably ended in divorce within a couple of years. Yvonne had to hide her secret visits to Sean when he was in jail. And when, upon his release, she had to reveal that they were a couple again, the

166

development did not go down well in their Clontarf home. Even though he was now their son-in-law and the father of the beautiful six year old granddaughter they doted upon, they still could not find a way to like him.

Having their daughter marry an 'ex-con' had not done their reputation in their respectable locality any good. The words 'Fraudster', 'Felon', 'Inmate' and 'Attempted Murderer' did not at all sit well with them, and by far outweighed the titles 'Successful Author' and 'Multi-Millionaire'. They could not hide their dislike of him, and were aghast when he cemented his relationship with Yvonne with a diamond and a daughter. They were relieved to learn that he would spare them societal embarrassment by not turning up at the family and friends event they had organised for Saturday evening in Dublin.

"Be good for Grandpa and Grandma, won't you?" urged Sean, "And show off your manners and all the nice words you learned at school". His little daughter nodded.
"And when you are up in the sky make sure you look down and see if you can see our house. I will be standing outside by the pool waving up at you!"
"I will Daddy" she replied. "But I looked out of my window earlier and it looks very cloudy up there, so I might not see you this time!"
"Tell Steven to fly the plane low so!" instructed the loving father gently, as he held her by both shoulders and placed a tender kiss on her forehead.
"I love you Admira" he whispered. "See you Sunday evening, OK?"
"And I love you too Daddy" she replied, kissing him on the lips as he knelt by her, "And I shall see you on Sunday evening too! And don't forget to feed Pebbles!"

"Bye Yvonne, take care over there!" said Sean as he kissed his glamorous looking wife. "I will collect ye on Sunday evening, text when ye arrive. And I hope you enjoy the party."
"I shall give them all your best wishes!" she smirked.
"Well as long as you don't give them my love!" he whispered into her ear. "I will save that for you on Sunday night!"

"You better!" she laughed as she took Admira by the hand and led her towards the door. "The landscaper is finishing up shortly so you will have the manor ALL to yourself shortly, M'Lord!"
"Peace at last!" replied her husband. "Have a nice weekend too, Morgan!"

Admira knelt on the back seat of the Daimler car and blew kisses to her waving father as they left their property. Sean turned and made for the giant front door of the house to resume his writing. But he was distracted by the sound of the music that was coming from the empty red van of the landscaper. It was a familiar sound. And as he drew nearer the van, he could clearly hear the distinctive sound of Lou Reed singing 'Perfect Day' – the song that was played at the end of Thomas Goy's funeral Mass. It was the first time that Sean had heard the track since, and a shudder reverberated through him as the American rock star ended the song with the haunting line:
"You're gonna reap just what you sow."

"Weird!" uttered the 37 year old to himself. "Where on earth did THAT song come from?" And for a moment his mind recalled the last time he heard that song in Ballycroy church, with Teeko to his left and Thomas's coffin to his right. An eerie feeling came over him. But Sean was able to shrug it off. "That song will be bouncing around in my head all day now. Damn it, how will I ever get any chapters done?!"

Sure enough, he found himself humming it as he decided to forego the writing and instead go through his September bank statements. He went to the red-walled kitchen at the rear of the mansion, where he could see the landscaper stooped in the rear lawn with his back to him. A wheelbarrow beside him. Sean spent about three quarters of an hour going through his statements from The Cayman Islands, Pretoria, Geneva, Luxembourg, The Jersey Islands and Gibraltar. Ralph had suggested an investment opportunity in China that Sean thought he ought to give some consideration to. He piled the statements on the middle of the table that faced the interior gable wall of the house. He calculated that he had £17 million at his disposal, but he had to go upstairs for his calculator so that he could convert some of the exchange rates more accurately.

Sean spent several minutes upstairs and when he was coming down he heard the back door being opened and footsteps in the kitchen. He thought that it must just be the landscaper coming in for hot water or something, but he rushed down the stairs as he did not want a stranger peering at his private statements.

As he came closer to the kitchen he could feel a slight chill coming into the hallway – the workman had obviously left the rear door open. "Bloody cheek!" Sean thought to himself, but he promised himself that he would remain friendly and calm to the man they were employing, the last thing he wanted to do was come across as one of those cantankerous upper class types!

He drew a deep breath as he entered the kitchen. Instead of glancing at the landscaper he looked disapprovingly over at the unclosed rear door. He then looked at his pile of documents in the middle of the table. And he then glared at the man sporting a heavy woollen hat who was sitting by that same table, with his back to the wall, facing the chair where Sean had been sitting. He appeared to be staring downwards but the writer deliberately avoided eye-contact as he was annoyed at this intrusion. He was miffed too about the landscaper sitting so close to the confidential information, but he bit his lip and marched over to the rear door which he slammed shut.

"Better keep the place warm or I might catch a cold!" he said, still avoiding eye contact, but making his way back to his chair.
"Sit thee down!" said the 'guest' firmly. Sean was taken aback. Was this the landscaper at all? Was it a robber? An intruder? He looked out at the garden but all he could see was the wheelbarrow. He looked again at the man sitting down in front of him, who was purposely hiding his face by staring downwards, his woolly hat obscuring his features.
"I said SIT THEE DOWN!" shouted the man, still looking down as he sat in his chair.
"How...how dare you!" stuttered Sean. "How fucking dare you! Who the hell do you think you..."

His sentence was stopped dead in its tracks as the head of the man looked up towards him. It was a face that Sean knew he recognised, but he could not believe what he was seeing. He could not believe WHO he was seeing. He felt himself slip into the chair and sit where he had been examining his bank statements. His eyes were fixed firmly on the person that sat across from him. He felt himself go impossibly freezing cold, like an iceberg.

The man sitting across the table from him smiled wickedly. His yellow teeth appeared from beneath his long narrow nose. Sean recognised the features of his grey-skinned visitor.

The man slowly drew up his right hand and pulled off his woolly hat, revealing his matted brownish greying hair. Sean recognised the floppy fringe. He recognised the eyes – despite the purplish rings around them. And he recognised the birthmark that seemed to be caked in a ghoulish mixture of crimson and dark red blood.

It was Thomas Goy.

Sean could not blink. His eyes were fixed on the grey face across from him. The smiling features that now appeared evil. He felt his heart pound against his chest. He felt the blood turn into frost in his veins. As with the visitations from Mary Beth, his limbs were paralysed. And his tongue dried. But differently, his teeth started to chatter involuntarily. Clattering together at a rapid rate. So loud that they hurt his ear drums.

After nearly two decades of spiritly experiences, Sean was experiencing the sight of an actual ghost for the first time. And it was horrendous. He was totally helpless. Gripped by an overwhelming fear. Thomas stared at him and continued smiling. But it was a sinister smile. His bloodshot eyes were glazed, but were dancing and demonic. But it was the bleeding birthmark on his forehead that was the most disturbing sight. As Sean tried and failed to blink, he was forced to watch helplessly as a trickle of blood descended slowly down the side of Thomas's pale face.

This was worse than any nightmare. It was actually happening. Thomas Goy was back to inflict his revenge. Sean wondered what was going to happen next. As the painful chattering in his own skull continued, he wondered if the ghost would speak again. He wondered if he should start to pray. But he could not think of a prayer.

"You can forget about praying!" snapped Thomas, "That will not work with me, Sean."
The terrified 37 year old was crippled with fear. A dead man was talking to him!

"And I know you are experiencing that awful clatter of your jaws, so I shall speak louder" continued Thomas, staring at his prey, not blinking. The chattering grew faster as Sean felt that his heart would expire as it was beating at least tenfold.

"YOU will listen to ME now, my 'friend'!" continued Thomas, his facial features contorting. Sean tried to nod but he couldn't. Other than his rattling jaws, he was a statue. His time was up. Death was at hand. He recalled Teeko seeing a ghost on his final day. It was now his turn. His very own Grim Reaper was sitting across from him. And his fate was decided.

"This very day, this very Friday, 17 years ago, YOU accompanied ME on my last journey. And YOU did ME wrong. By sticking out your cursed thumb you halted my earthly existence. And now, as promised that dreadful day of my death, I am back to not only gain revenge on the man who wronged me, but to surpass that. You remember that promise, don't you? No need to respond, I know that you can not!"

Sean's chattering continued...

"YOU are a thief. You thieved from my parents. You thieved from my brother. You thieved from my bride-to-be. You thieved from my friend Norman. You thieved from my diary. You thieved from my writing. You thieved from my wallet. You thieved from my female friends. And yet you stood by my grave and cried. You asked for a sign. I hope you are happy now. You were not worthy

171

of being visited in a dream. This, today, better serves my purpose!"

Sean's chattering continued...

"You will try to shed tears as I tell you what I have done, but you will be unable cry. Even though you will plunge to depths of sadness that you did not think imaginable. Beneath this pile of your ill-attained millions lies your pistol. You will have just about enough energy left to pull its trigger and end this deceptive life of yours."

Sean's chattering continued. He knew the end was on its way. His heart ached as he wondered what Thomas was about to inflict. He imagined the faces of his wife and child should they return and find him dead by suicide. He wanted to cry out but he couldn't. He was riveted to the kitchen chair. He was overcome by an indescribable sadness.

"At this very moment, your wife and child are taking their final breaths. Breaths full of water, as their plane has dropped from the sky and entered the channel."

Those words sorrowfully pierced the frozen heart of Sean shattering it into a million shards as his soul cried aloud to the Gods. But no one heard his cries. The thought of his beautiful little six year old and her mother dying hurt more than words could imagine. He tried to cry but he was paralysed. He tried to blink but he could not. The only movement in his body was the chattering at an ever-increasing rate.

All of his millions could not prevent him from yearning for the moment when he could use his gun to put an end to his pain. Images of his beloved girls perishing in the cold sea filled his mind. He could see the horror in Admira's tiny face as they realised the little plane was nose-diving. He could see his crying wife reaching out to try and cradle her beloved daughter as the craft neared the water. Their screams filled his head along with the awful chattering. This was the moment that he wanted to cuddle his girls the most – and the moment that they needed a cuddle from their strong protective man the most. But the three of them were helpless. How could Thomas be so cruel? To take an innocent little girl away, his angel Admira? And to take the divine Yvonne in her prime?

"NOW you might be beginning to experience some of the pain I experienced as Ursula howled at my grave, thinking I did not love her" continued Thomas with his ghostly monologue. "When she pleaded with me to return and save her from herself. NOW you might be beginning to experience some of the grief my poor mother, father and brother had to endure. NOW you might be beginning to feel some of the torture Norman felt as he was locked up with lunatics because of you. NOW you might be beginning to feel some of the heartbreak you wrought within Jacqueline and Debbie, my friends."

Sean's chattering continued. He felt he was beginning to lose consciousness. He wanted to respond but of course there was no chance of that....

"I feel your pain for little Admira" said Thomas solemnly. "She did not deserve a father like you. That poor girl is destined NEVER to reach the age of seven upon this forsaken earth. Don't you realise – Admira IS the spirit you called Mary Beth. You ceased having visitations once she was conceived. Did you not make that connection? Did this great intelligence that served you so well in replicating my work fail on this occasion? She again made her away onto this earth through you, but sadly the little one's eternal purgatory continues. We both know that the Irish Famine saw her die at six from starvation. Before that, Cromwell and The Black Death were her fate. Before that again she died horrendous deaths through human sacrifice and witchcraft. Now she dies in a capsule submerged beneath the sea. As Admira. But unlike you, she WILL be back. In another time. In another guise. With another name. But YOU will NEVER be back! There is only one place you are going, you Heathen! Let thee roast there for eternity!"

The hellish chattering continued and was wearing Sean out, eroding the last of his energy. His jaws were in immense pain as his upper and lower teeth clashed for the millionth time. But his wicked visitor was not yet finished with his tirade:

"You stole my work and enjoyed many vices with my wealth. You imbibed alcohol. You abused women. You used prostitutes. You lied. You squandered. You gambled. You gorged. You defiled. You masqueraded. You sodomized. You will now pay eternally for taking advantage of me – Thomas Goy. Have you not made the connection yet between my name and my purpose? Has your great intellect failed yet again, I ask? Have you not deduced that the nine letters that make up my name 'Thomas Goy' also spell the words 'Mayo Ghost'? No, you did not! We can see now why you had to thieve the talents of others to progress on this earth. Well, 17 years to the day it has come full circle – and just as you were the last person to see me off, so shall I be the last to see you off." And he slowly extended his left arm and clenched his grey skinned fist, before raising his thumb in the manner that Sean had signalled in Dublin exactly 17 years earlier.

By now Sean's chattering was coming to an end. His facial muscles were simply unable to meet the demand. He felt exhausted, as the ice cold feeling left his body and he felt feeble power pipe back into his legs and feet. He felt a tear trickle down his cheek as he turned his head and saw a happy photograph of him and his wife and child laughing; beside a painting that Admira had done for him at school. As he entered his final minute in the world all that filled his numbed senses was the terrifying expressions and screams of his frightened six year old and her 36 year old equally petrified mother. Sean knew that he had been beaten. Payback was here. He could not face this world without his two beloved girls. The pain was too much to bear. He clambered for his weapon beneath the sheets of paper as the ghost stood up and gazed down at him, before speaking again:

"You even had the effrontery to use my line 'don't just get even – get ahead' as a title of your best seller. That was meant to be MINE, you swine! NOW you know what I meant. And I am glad to have my revenge. Besides young Admira, my other regret is that you did not have to carry this burden on this earth for the next 17 years. But we all knew that you were not man enough.

174

That you find it easier to take instead of make. That you find it easier to run away than to face the day. Be gone with you! May you suffer for eternity in the hellish hovel that awaits thee!"

As the phantom figure of the Mayo Ghost disappeared into the unknown, a single gunshot echoed through the Reigate countryside and the red kitchen walls of the McRobert kitchen became even redder. The last line that Sean was ever to read was the quote that he had tattooed into his forearm *"My Mama says, to get things done, you better not mess with Major Tom."* S.R. McRobert had paid a high price for messing with the world of the dead. And for messing with the deceased Tom Goy.

No book could do justice to the cruel sufferings inflicted on Sean and his loved ones on that fateful October Friday in the year 2013. The off-duty Daithí Donaghy sobbed unashamedly on his large couch and tightly clasped his wife and two children as Sky News broke news of the McRobert family tragedy, his light blue collar turning navy from the tears that rolled from his eyes. The planned party in Dublin became a wailing wake as the Griffins grieved the tragic loss of their gorgeous girls. The county of Mayo mourned for a famous son. Even the trembling skeletal Norman O'Toole wept as he watched the television coverage alone in his cold County Kerry cottage.

If only young Sean McRobert had heeded the chilling warning of his Mayo Ghost exactly 17 years earlier. Unfortunately he had not, and his greedy disrespectful opportunism had unleashed hell upon many innocent people – the latest of these being his adored wife, his cherished little girl and his loyal pilot Steven. And his actions had unleashed hell upon those left on earth who loved them – creating a valley of tears.

From beyond the grave, Thomas Goy had got ahead. Again.

"Now I know what a ghost is. Unfinished business, that's what."
Salman Rushdie, The Satanic Verses.

ACKNOWLEDGEMENTS

To my wife Laura – for your unwavering loyalty, support, patience and love. Thank you for making all of my dreams come true.

To Leah and Eva – sorry for not spending enough time on YOUR books! Keep up the reading, writing, drawing and colouring.

To my parents John and Irene – thank you for EVERYTHING.

To Patrick, Gary, Helen and all of your families – I treasure your support, and the fact that you are always there for me.

To the extended Ginty and Rowland families – thank you for your loyalty and encouragement.

To all of my friends in Mayo, Limerick and beyond – I am honoured by knowing you all. If only we could get to spend more time together...

To the Fitzpatrick Family in Limerick – thank you for embracing me into your clan. It means so much.

To Majella and Paul – your kindness knows no bounds and the girls and I are so fortunate to have you in our lives.

To Aoife Murray and Patricia McDermott – your immense professional assistance will always be gratefully appreciated. Take a bow.

To Bridget Cafferkey and Mary Mika – thank you for leading the effort to spread the word overseas. And we haven't even met yet!

To David Brennan, Sharon Bunce, Andrew Haworth and Claire O'Donovan – I could not have done this without your expertise and professionalism – which is always entwined with genuine care and support.

To the wonderful community of Ballycroy – your warmth follows your sons and daughters far beyond your borders - and always inspires.

To all who read this book - I hope you enjoyed the trip! I would welcome your feedback on the Mayo Ghost facebook page. Thank you.